*A
Harlequin
Romance*

OTHER
Harlequin Romances
by ISOBEL CHACE

THE
CORNISH HEARTH

by

ISOBEL CHACE

HARLEQUIN BOOKS   TORONTO
WINNIPEG

Harlequin edition published August 1975

SBN 373-01904-1

Original hard cover edition published in 1975
by Mills & Boon Limited.

All the characters in this book have no existence outside the
imagination of the Author, and have no relation whatsoever to
anyone bearing the same name or names. They are not even
distantly inspired by any individual known or unknown to the
Author, and all the incidents are pure invention.

Printed in Canada

1904

Who pent up the sea behind closed doors when it leapt tumultuous out of the womb, when I wrapped it in a robe of mist and made black clouds its swaddling bands; when I marked the bounds it was not to cross and made it fast with a bolted gate? Come thus far, I said, and no farther; here your proud waves shall break.

The Book of Job: 38:8-11

CHAPTER ONE

ANNA ST. JAMES blinked as she stepped out of the taxi and walked on to the lit platform at Paddington Station. Before her stood the night train to Penzance, shutters closed and with only the doors at the ends of the carriages standing open to give it some sign of life.

"Penzance?" the porter asked her. "That'll be Platform One. Your name will be on the door."

Together they wandered down the platform checking each list as they came to it. About halfway down the train she found her name and the porter stowed her luggage away in the sleeping compartment that had been allotted to her. Anna gave him a tip and then sat down on the bunk and looked about her, marvelling at the compactness and the planning that had gone into such a small place. She had not travelled first class for such a long time and she found it frankly exciting.

It was two years almost to the day since her ailing mother had finally died. Anna had found it a hard struggle to support her mother when she had been alive, and lonely after her death; so lonely that she had concentrated fiercely on her job, finding to her surprise that she had become a minor celebrity in her own field. For Anna designed jewellery of the modern, chunky sort, made from various pebbles or semi-precious stones, the kind of thing that anyone can afford, that is pretty and spectacular without being in the least bit valuable. Most of the famous London stores took samples of her work now, and this had encouraged Anna to think that she was well enough known to leave London. In Cornwall, the county which had been her mother's home, she could find her own materials and make up the jewellery, sending it in batches to the London stores who would continue to deal with her. And now, at last, this dream was becoming a reality and by morning she would have arrived in Penzance with all Cornwall at her feet

It was cold in the night. Anna had opened her window as wide as it would go, and had pulled the screen to one side so that she could see out. There was something luxurious, she thought, about lying in bed and watching the countryside pass by outside, even in the dark.

She slept fitfully, only half aware when they pulled into Exeter and later on into Plymouth. But when, about an hour later, they moved slowly out of Devon and across the Tamar into Cornwall, she was wide awake, anxious to get her first glimpse of the county from the famous Saltash Bridge. It was still dark, despite it being June, but the night was grey rather than black, as if the day would break at any moment, flooding the countryside with light.

And so it was. She sat up in her bunk and watched the scenery flash past her, admiring the wild rhododendrons that flowered on the banks and the occasional glimpses of sea. By the time they had reached the great white mounds of waste that surrounded the areas of the clay industry the sun had come out. Anna, intrigued by the floury appearance of the buildings, began to dress When she had finished, she opened the door into the corridor so that she could see out on both sides of the train, and rang the bell for the attendant to bring her morning tea.

"What time do we get to Penzance?" she asked him when he came

He glanced at his watch. "At about a quarter past eight. You have plenty of time, madam," he assured her.

She smiled ruefully. "It isn't that," she admitted. "I shall need all the time I can get in Penzance this morning. I haven't yet found anywhere to stay. I'm going to spend the whole summer here, you see."

"You've left it a bit late!" he exclaimed. "Cornwall is apt to fill up in the summer."

"I know," Anna admitted lazily. "But if you're going to spend the whole summer in a place, it doesn't pay to buy a pig in a poke!"

"No, madam," the attendant agreed doubtfully. "Would you be thinking of buying, then?"

Anna made a face at him, thoughtfully pouring out her tea. "I may do – in the end," she said. "It depends."

The attendant smiled at her. She was a pleasure to look at, he thought, with her startlingly blonde hair and easy ways. He regretted that he had to leave her to serve his other passengers. He would have felt easier if she hadn't told him that she had nowhere to stay. She was the kind to be taken in, and he thought it was a pity. A decent tipper too, he thought with approval as he took her tray from her and noted the amount she had quietly put under the saucer. He hoped she would fall on her feet, but to come to Cornwall in the summer without making proper arrangements was downright improvident.

"I hope you find somewhere, madam."

She laughed. "Oh, I will! It isn't the season yet!"

The attendant wished he were half as confident, but he had forgotten all about her as he made his way down the corridor, collecting up the tea-trays as he went. He yawned. It had been a long night and he would be glad when it was over.

When he had gone, Anna sat back, determined to enjoy the last of the journey. She recognised Hayle at once, and was surprised to remember the two names of the divided town. Foundry and Copperhouse: names that showed how deeply the tin mines had bitten into Cornish life and history. She remembered too how Hayle came from the old Cornish word

9

meaning estuary. How odd, she thought, that she should have remembered such a thing after all this time.

It seemed no time after that that she caught a glimpse of St. Michael's Mount out of the corridor window and knew that in a few minutes she would be in Penzance. Excitement knotted within her and, to give herself something to do, she went out and stood in the corridor, watching the sea that was streaked with navy blue and emerald green and looking quiet and amenable under the clear light of the early morning sun.

When the train stopped, Anna went back to her apartment and piled her luggage neatly on the bunk. She took a quick look at herself in the looking-glass, annoyed by the sprinkling of freckles that decorated the bridge of her nose. Quickly, she smothered them with powder and put on some more lipstick for good measure. When she had done, she was still not satisfied. Her dark grey eyes seemed to her to dominate her face, giving her a fragile look that had no relation to the truth. She sighed, wishing that the years of looking after herself that she had gone through had left her with a less vulnerable appearance. It was so easily misunderstood!

"Porter, ma'am?" a voice asked her through the open door.

She pointed to her suitcases. "Can you take it to the left luggage office?" she asked him.

"I will. Follow me up when you're ready," he answered.

It was a long platform. Anna gazed around her, expecting to remember it all from her childhood, but it was strange and completely unfamiliar. She handed in her ticket and stood, indecisively, beside the barrier, wondering what to do next. The porter waved to her and she began to go across to him when she came face to face with a man who was vaguely familiar to her. She half-smiled at him in case she did indeed know him, for he was tall and elegant and quite extraordinarily attractive to her. She was rewarded by an amused grin, almost as if he

10

nad been expecting her.

"What a happy coincidence!" he murmured.

She raised her eyebrows haughtily. "Coincidence?" she repeated.

"You told me you would be on the train," he said certainly. "I should have thought you would have remembered."

Remember she did with sudden and humiliating completeness. Temper blazed within her. *How dared he!* Oh yes, she remembered him now! It had been in London that she had seen him. She had had an appointment with the buyer of a wholesale firm who had been mounting an exhibition of Cornish wares throughout their line of shops. Anna had duly found herself in the office of a Miss Bryant, a fierce, bespectacled female, whose shapeless dress said little for her personal good taste. There had followed an uncomfortable half hour as Miss Bryant had refused to believe that Anna's jewellery was authentically Cornish, either in their design or material. And then *this man* had walked into the office and the formidable Miss Bryant had gushingly included him in the argument.

"This – er – young lady," she had said, "is offering us some of her jewellery for *our* exhibition. I am trying to explain to her that we can only accept authentic pieces *from Cornwall –*"

The man had looked amused. "Are you Cornish?" he had asked Anna.

"Not exactly," she had admitted.

Miss Bryant had preened herself. "That was what I was pointing out –"

"My mother was a Cornish woman," Anna had continued firmly. "As a matter of fact I'm going to live there myself – in Penzance. I'm taking the night train on Tuesday week."

"That's quite beside the point," Miss Bryant had said grandly. "We are very pleased to be having the help of St. Piran's Society of Cornish Men and Women with this exhi-

11

bition, and I would be failing in my duty if I were to accept *anything* that wasn't truly Cornish –"

"You haven't seen my jewellery yet," Anna had reminded her steadily. She was terribly aware that in any other circumstances she would have welcomed the faint look of interest in the man's eyes. As it was, she was only conscious that not only was he the last person she would have chosen to have witnessed this particular interview, which from her point of view was hardly going well, but that he was also in some indefinable way an ally of the terrible Miss Bryant.

"I don't need to," Miss Bryant said smugly. "It isn't Cornish and that's that! I'm sorry, Miss – er, but I can't allow you to waste Mr. Trethowyn's time like this. Good morning."

Anna had given her a look of contempt. "And do you agree with her?" she had demanded of the man.

He had looked as though he were enjoying himself. "I agree that we can only show truly Cornish exhibits in this exhibition," he had said mildly.

She had been furiously angry. "And that doesn't include me?"

He had grinned. "I think you'd make a very decorative exhibit!" he had retorted, tongue in cheek.

If he had been less attractive, she would have been less angry. She had picked up her case of samples, said good-bye to Miss Bryant in withering tones, and had made her departure. The man's manners had been impeccable, she remembered with a distinctly lowering feeling. He had held the door for her, had bowed slightly as she had swept through it, and had said: "See you in Penzance, I hope."

And now here he was, as attractive as ever, and she could only glower at him in remembered humiliation and wish she were dead.

"I don't think I caught your name?" he was saying easily.

12

Anna frowned. "We weren't introduced!" she said sharply.

He looked amused. "Miss Bryant is the overpowering type, don't you think?" he observed kindly. "I can see that she's not easily to be forgotten, but can I give you a lift somewhere?"

"Thank you, no," she said with dignity. She wondered what he was doing on Penzance Station at that hour of the morning. He bothered her, there was no doubt about it, for he made her doubly aware of the freckles on her nose and even more conscious that she had nowhere to go until she had found herself a room somewhere. The porter had grown tired of waiting. She could see him hovering in the background and she turned to him with a feeling of relief.

"You did say the left luggage, miss?" the porter reminded her, making it clear with a vivid gesture of his head that there were other passengers waiting for his services.

"Yes, I did. Thank you," she said. She was bitterly aware that she was blushing and hoped against hope that the man, whoever he was, would go away and leave her to her own devices.

But the man obviously had no intention of doing anything of the sort. "The left luggage office?" he said, raising an eyebrow in amused enquiry.

Anna turned her wide, grey eyes full on him. "Look," she said, "do you think you could possibly mind your own business?"

He laughed. "Not possibly!" he retorted. He waved a couple of coins at the porter. "Put the bags in my car, will you?" he said.

Anna strove silently to control her temper. "I have no intention of going anywhere with you!" she snapped, annoyed by her own lack of resolution.

The man took base advantage of her dilemma. "Where else are you going?" he asked simply. "There's no need to look so

13

worried! I have no intention of kidnapping you, simply to drive you to wherever it is that you're going."

"I'm not going anywhere!" she muttered, cornered.

She thought his surprise was rather overdone. "Oh?" he prompted her.

"I haven't quite settled where I'm going to live," she added mutinously.

"Then you've nothing to lose by coming with me, have you?" he said soothingly.

She was of the opinion that she had a great deal to lose, but she had just enough common sense not to say so. Instead, she allowed herself to be led out into the car park and settled herself into the front seat of a car that looked both expensive and well used.

"Are you hungry?" he asked her, as he got into the car beside her. "I hope you are, for nothing gives Ellen greater pleasure than visitors."

Ellen, Anna presumed, was the man's wife.

He drove easily through the rather complicated one-way system of roads and through Penzance. Anna was glad that he was silent for a moment, for she wanted to look about her, to try to remember the streets where her mother had been brought up and where she had, though only once, come for a long-remembered holiday. The mock-Egyptian architecture startled her. She was amused by the sight of so many Nefertitis holding up the façade of the newly painted building. She had no recollection of seeing such a building before, but she did remember the statue of Sir Humphry Davy, holding the safety lamp he had invented for miners.

They left Penzance, climbing steeply up a country lane with banks on either side, built up with golden-grey stone and covered with pennywort and a variety of other flowers that had, some time or other, escaped from a neighbouring garden. At

14

the top of the hill they came into the village proper, grouped about the church and public house.

"I live just round the corner," the man said suddenly, as they waited for the green bus to reverse into the narrow square, to turn round and return to Penzance.

"Here in Penwith?" Anna exclaimed.

He looked at her curiously. "Why not?" he asked.

She didn't know why not. There was something about him, about the air he wore so easily that he had been born to command, and something about his manners, that had led her to suppose that he lived in a mansion rather than a cottage, such as the cottages she could see all round her.

"Have you always lived here?" she countered.

"Always!" he agreed with pride.

He had reason to be proud, she thought, for, when they turned the corner he had pointed out to her, the stone bank gave way to a wall that had been coloured cream a few years before, but which had now faded to the colour of Jersey milk and was impregnated with patterns of dust. Here and there, the rendering had fallen away entirely, to allow some plant to cling precariously to the layers of dust that had fallen behind it. Above the wall, she could see an enormous fig tree growing, the leaves waving gently in the breeze.

So it was a mansion after all! She noted with approval the palm trees at the entrance and the flame tree that guarded the kitchen door. The house had been built with its back to the road so that the main rooms could benefit from the splendid view that took in the whole of Mount's Bay, dominated by the ancient stronghold of St. Michael's Mount.

"So this is where you live!" Anna said softly.

He eyed her warily. "The Trethowyns have always lived here," he said, the pride of centuries in his voice.

"That's what I suspected," Anna murmured. She was

15

amused that he had apparently been teased so seldom. "It has a settled look about it," she added.

"Settled?" he repeated suspiciously.

She poked her tongue out at him and as quickly withdrew it. "I didn't like to say complacent," she explained meekly.

"I should hope not!" he retorted. "You'd better come inside and meet my son and heir. By the way, now that you know my name may I know yours?"

"I'm Anna St. James," she told him.

He looked at her for a long moment. "It suits you," he said. "Do you mind if we go through the kitchen?"

She shook her head. She was seldom envious of anyone else's possessions, but this house was something such as she had often dreamed about. It was true that the buildings could do with a fresh coat of paint, but the orchards were immaculately kept and the gardens were lovely, lovelier than any she had ever seen before. There were great splashes of crimson mesembryanthemum, foxgloves, gladioli, and a hundred other flowers, some of which she had never seen before.

"Mr. Piran? Is that you? Was the young lady on the train? The boy has been asking for you."

Mr. Trethowyn opened the kitchen door. "Yes, it's me, Ellen. I've brought her back to breakfast. Can we have it on the verandah?"

The woman who greeted them certainly wasn't Mr. Trethowyn's wife. She was as dark as any Spaniard, her hair prematurely grey and her face lined and weathered by the sun. Her eyes were black rather than brown, half hidden by hooded eyelids that were apt to hide her thoughts from those she was talking to. And yet she was not Spanish. If she was foreign at all she was only foreign in the same way as all Cornwall stands apart from the rest of England.

"The boy is not up yet," she said.

16

"I'll see to him," Mr. Trethowyn offered. "Will you look after Miss St. James?"

Ellen looked Anna up and down with the obvious curiosity of the countrywoman. "Sit down, Miss St. James," she said. "Mr. Piran will be a few minutes with the boy. It will be more interesting for you to wait for him here before going through to the verandah."

Anna smiled at her. "Is the boy his son?" she said.

Ellen nodded. "His name is Peter."

"And his mother?" Anna pressed her.

"Dead. She went away down the line to London." She lowered her voice. "She never told *him* she was going. She was killed there in a traffic accident. There's some that says it's just as well, for she wasn't coming back. But I wouldn't know about that, for it was before I came. Now there's only Mr. Piran and the boy."

Anna swallowed. She felt she had been told more than Mr. Trethowyn could possibly have wished her to know.

"And how old is Peter?" she asked brightly.

"Thirteen."

Anna glanced surreptitiously at her watch. It was nearly half-past nine. How odd she thought that the boy wasn't at school. Perhaps he wasn't very well? She reminded herself firmly that it was none of her business, but it nagged at the back of her mind all the time she was waiting for Mr. Trethowyn to reappear.

"I expect you could do with some splits and cream after your bacon and eggs," Ellen said comfortably. "That's what most people come to Cornwall for, isn't it?"

Anna was surprised. "Do they? I've come to work here."

"There's not much work about here," Ellen said bluntly.

Anna chuckled. "I've brought my own with me! I make jewellery out of pebbles and semi-precious stones."

17

"Then you've come to the right place. The boy has quite a collection of stones and things he has found for himself on the beach. He has a piece of rose quartz that came up after a storm that he's particularly proud of. You'd better ask him if you can see it."

"Yes, I will." Anna was immediately interested. "I'd love to see what he has. It will give me a clue as to what I can expect to find myself."

Ellen's black eyes snapped at her across the table. "And Mr. Piran?" she asked. "What does he have to do with your coming?"

Anna blushed. "Nothing!" she insisted quickly.

"He went to meet your train," Ellen reminded her.

"Did he really?" Anna felt more uncomfortable than ever. "But we've never really met! I was trying to sell some jewellery to a buyer in London and he came in and sided with her over the fact that my work wasn't truly Cornish," she went on with remembered bitterness.

"And you minded?" Ellen suggested.

"No," Anna said untruthfully. Was it possible that he had really gone to Penzance specially to meet her train? "I don't suppose he knows anything about Cornish jewellery!"

"You'd be wrong there," Ellen said soberly. "Mr. Piran does a great deal to forward the interests of Cornwall. He encourages tourism and Cornish industries –"

"St. Piran's Society of Cornish Men and Women?" Anna put in curiously.

Ellen nodded. "He works harder than most –"

Anna's eyes kindled. "With his own society to boot!" she observed.

Ellen sniffed. "You could say that. I can hear the boy coming," she added. "I'll show you the way through to the verandah."

Her ears must have been very acute, for Anna had heard nothing, but she stood up and followed Ellen into the hall and through the shabby sitting-room where the moulded ceilings and the vast proportions showed a grandeur that even the torn covers to the chairs couldn't conceal. Ellen pushed open the french windows and Anna stepped out on to the verandah. Ahead of her stretched the garden and beyond that Mount's Bay. The sheer beauty of it made her catch her breath and wonder that anyone should live all their lives in such lovely surroundings.

She only slowly became aware that she was being watched. She turned her back to the view and came face to face with a young boy seated in a wheel-chair. His face was white under a mop of blue-black hair and it looked as if it had been a long time since he had laughed or enjoyed anything very much.

"Peter?" Anna said uncertainly.

The boy nodded briefly. "There's no need to feel sorry for me," he began in stilted tones.

"Certainly not!" Anna agreed placidly.

The boy actually smiled. "I like you," he announced. "Piran said I might."

"Why do you call him Piran?" Anna asked him.

The boy gave her a scornful look. "It's his name," he said unanswerably.

'I thought it might be a nickname," Anna defended herself. "I've never heard it before. I thought it was 'pirate' at first. *That* would have been very suitable!" she added with feeling.

The boy was shocked. "Never heard of Piran!" he repeated. "He's the patron saint of Cornwall."

"Oh," said Anna.

"Didn't you know?" he asked curiously.

Anna shook her head. "No, I didn't," she said.

The boy wheeled himself over to the table and sat moodily

gazing out at the sea, her presence apparently forgotten. When Piran Trethowyn stepped out of the sitting-room to join them his son was still sitting there his shoulders hunched and his eyes firmly fixed on St. Michael's Mount.

"Are you hungry?" Mr. Trethowyn asked Anna. "Ellen is just coming."

The boy turned suddenly. "Where are you going to live?" he demanded bluntly of Anna.

"I don't know yet," she replied easily. "I want a room with a workshop attached."

Peter turned his head to look at his father. "Chyanbara!" he blurted out.

Mr. Trethowyn shook his head. "It's in a bad state of repair," he said.

"It's not bad!" his son insisted. "It has this old Cornish hearth," he explained to Anna. "Chyanbara means the bread house. That's because it still has this bread oven in the hearth. It's empty now," he added with a sigh.

Anna glanced uncertainly at the boy's father. The man shook his head. "It isn't what you want," he said certainly.

The boy's face turned red with anger. "It is! It is! I'll show her the house myself!"

"All right!" Mr. Trethowyn almost shouted at him. "You can do as you like!"

"I think I'd rather find somewhere for myself," Anna put in uncertainly.

Mr. Trethowyn shrugged. "Suit yourself!" he said almost sulkily. He went to help Ellen with the breakfast things, placing the hot dishes carefully on the table. When he had done, his face cleared and he smiled. It was like the sun coming out after rain – or like living on a roller coaster, Anna told herself wryly. Both Trethowyns were moody and ill-tempered, she thought. They made a good match for each other!

Anna had not known that she was hungry, but she found the eggs and bacon so tasty and the bread and butter so fresh that she had eaten her fair share of the food almost before she was aware. Peter, on the other hand, did no more than play with his breakfast, and she had the feeling that he was only present at the meal at all to please his father. At the first possible moment, he wheeled his chair away from the table and out into the garden.

"Haven't you finished yet?" he asked Anna impatiently. "I want to show you the house."

Mr. Trethowyn gave no sign that he heard his son. Anna watched him help himself to some of the clotted cream.

"I suppose it won't do any harm to look," she said.

Mr. Trethowyn grunted. "You're pretty enough to attract him!" he told her flatly.

Anna's own temper flared. "I suppose if I look at that remark for long enough, I might find a compliment in it!"

To her surprise he laughed. "You might indeed! Come on, we'll both show you the house, seeing that the boy is so set on it. But it isn't very comfortable, I warn you. The last tenant only died recently and I've had no time to do more than scrub the place out."

They walked almost companionably down the garden path with Peter going before them at a pace that terrified Anna in case he turned his chair over. She didn't notice the house at first. A fuchsia hedge almost hid it from the big house, the dangling ballerina flowers dancing in the breeze. There was a small gap in the hedge through which Peter went headlong and there, set in a tiny garden of its own, stood the two-roomed cottage.

It was built of stone with a slate roof that had been covered with thin concrete to render it more waterproof. The windows were low in the walls, and to enter at all one had to stoop almost double to get in the door. Inside there was no more than a concrete floor and simple whitewashed walls. The ancient hearth was the one remarkable feature, taking up almost half of the room with the oven at the back. A wooden settle stood along one side of it and a tall-backed wooden chair sat beside it.

"People don't like these hearths nowadays," Peter said fiercely, daring her to prefer anything more modern.

Anna stood in silence staring at the room. To her it was like a dream come true. Her eyes filled with tears and she blinked quickly in case they would think her a fool.

"What's in the other room?" she asked.

"The bedroom," Mr. Trethowyn said patiently. "There's a small space for cooking and washing at the back. The loo is at the end of the garden –"

Anna joined her hands together and turned and faced him. "How much rent would you want for it?" she burst out.

Mr. Trethowyn looked embarrassed. "Lord," he said, "I don't know! You'll have to ask the boy. It's his place really."

"It belongs to the Trethowyn heir," Peter explained gravely. "We'd better go back to the house and get your things."

"But I might not be able to afford –" Anna began hesitantly.

The boy looked as sulky as he had before. "I've said you can have it!" he insisted.

Anna stole another glance at the hearth and smiled. "Then behold your new tenant!" she said.

CHAPTER TWO

Mr. Trethowyn carried her suitcases down to the cottage, putting them down just inside the door.

"Rather you than me!" he commented grimly.

Anna hesitated. "I'm sorry if you don't like the arrangement," she said.

"The boy wants it, so it's all right with me," he answered.

He looked anything but pleased with the arrangement. Anna thought of his ambivalent attitude towards her coming to Cornwall at all and felt a certain sympathy for him. It was hard for him to end up with her on his doorstep.

"Why do you always call him 'the boy'?" she asked irrelevantly.

He was startled. "I don't know," he said. "I suppose my wife and I always talked about him like that. He was about the only thing we had in common," he added abruptly.

Anna said nothing. Poor Peter, she thought. "Will he always be confined to a wheelchair?" she asked aloud.

"We're hoping not. I don't think it worries him much."

Was he really so insensitive? Anna wondered. She hoped not. Peter deserved better than that. He was a strange boy, oddly adult for his years of full bravado and yet, she suspected, wretchedly unhappy underneath. He made a strange landlord!

"The cottage used to be let the old way," he had told her. "It was just a patch of ground which the tenant was allowed to live on by the landlord. He picked on any three people he liked, but when all three were dead the property reverted to the landlord. The lives were up years ago on this cottage, but

Piran wouldn't turn the old lady out because of it." Peter had laughed abruptly. "I think that's the way I'll let the cottage to you!"

"Indeed you won't!" Anna had told him flatly.

"It's the Cornish way!" he had remarked sulkily.

"In *this* century?" she had teased him gently.

He had shrugged his shoulders. "I wish I hadn't said you could have it," he had said crossly,

"Then I'll go away!" Anna had retorted, forgetting until it was too late how easily she lost her own temper and that she didn't want to go away.

Peter had smiled reluctantly. "Four pounds a week?" he had offered.

She had shaken hands with him. "Done," she had said.

"Did people really form a kind of tontine over the leases of their houses?" Anna asked Piran now.

"It was a bad system," he answered. "It was over the land really. The tenant built his own house. The landlord claimed everything when the last 'life' died, though. It was one of the ways the tinners had of finding somewhere to live. He was an independent fellow and didn't have much truck with the land-owners." He gave her an engaging grin. "The Trethowyns were land owners originally, but we made all our money in tin like the Godolphins, the Bassets, and most of the old Cornish families. Not that there's much money left now!" he added.

"But the land is still yours?"

"Some of it. I've sold off most of it. People get their tin from Malaya these days."

"And what do you do now?" she asked him.

He looked genuinely surprised. "Don't you know?" he said.

She shook her head. "Only that you represent St. Piran's Society. Is that a full-time job?"

24

He gave her an amused, thoughtful look. "It keeps me fairly busy. I have to keep the Miss Bryants of this world interested in all things Cornish. That's quite an undertaking on its own!"

"But they can't *all* have such little sense or taste!" she grunted.

"Nor do they all wield their power with such little sensitivity," he added with feeling.

"It didn't matter," Anna said awkwardly.

"And I'm forgiven?" he prompted her.

She laughed despite herself. "If you want to be," she agreed. She accepted his outstretched hand, mildly surprised that any kind of truce between them should matter so much to her. "I – I think I'll unpack," she said hurriedly, retrieving her hand from his warm, strong touch.

"Okay," he said, "I'll leave you to it."

When he had gone, she thought that she still didn't know much about him. She had to admit being curious. He was so sure of himself and, although his possessions were shabby, they were all expensive. She couldn't imagine him living as an impoverished country gentlemen in any circumstances and yet he didn't seem to have much money for his immediate use. It was all very puzzling.

She soon forgot all about the Trethowyns, however, in her pleasure in her new home. Now she was alone she was longing to explore the small cottage, or 'cabin' as Peter had called it. She sat on the wooden settle and hugged herself with glee that she had fallen on her feet in such a spectacular way. It was so exactly right and so exactly what she wanted!

Only the front of the cottage had been built of granite, she noticed. The back of the house was made of cob – a mixture of straw and glutinous clay. The floor, she supposed, had once been beaten earth, but had since been concreted over to keep out the damp. The furniture was old-fashioned, without much comfort, but the walls had been recently whitewashed and the copper pots on the wall had been newly polished and gleamed with friendly warmth in the dim light that struggled through the low windows.

The hearth was the feature that pleased her most of all. Built into the enormously thick wall, the original fireback was still in place and over it hung a cauldron made of solid iron. Behind, right at the back of the hearth, was the old bread oven. With some difficulty she opened it, to find it was oval in shape and marked with the sign of the cross to bless the bread that was baked inside it. There were also four curious marks on the door which Anna presumed had been put there to show the size of loaves it would bake. Although it was obvious that it hadn't been used for years, the oven was beautifully made and satisfying in the way that really beautiful tools always are.

Anna was just closing the oven door again when she heard footsteps outside the door. She looked over her shoulder to see who it was, but the footsteps came to a stop outside the door.

"Who is it?" she called out.

There was a long silence during which she pulled herself up on to her feet and walked slowly over to the door. She could only see the man outside from his waist downwards, so low was the door, and she was forced to stoop to see his face.

"Do you want something?" she asked him.

The stranger stooped also and doffed his hat. "I think I must have made some mistake," he said. "I was told this was Chyanbara, the home of Mrs. Austin."

"It is Chyanbara," Anna agreed. "Perhaps Mrs. Austin was the old lady who did live here? If so, I think she died recently."

The stranger seemed unaffected by this piece of news. He smiled cheerfully, patting his immaculate trousers with a tanned hand. "This isn't a very comfortable way to conduct a conversation, is it? Do you think I might come in?"

Anna stepped back to allow him through the low doorway. "I've only just arrived," she explained, flustered by her visitor's appearance. He was too beautiful for a man, though he gave no sign of trading on his good looks. "You would do better to go up to the big house."

"I'm very contented to talk to you!" he smiled. "My name is Michael Vaynor, by the way."

"I'm Anna St. James."

"Anna? That's a pretty name – almost as pretty as you are! How did you persuade Piran to let you the cottage?"

Anna looked down at her fingers. "Do you know the Trethowyns?" she asked.

Michael Vaynor laughed. "I ought to! Piran is my brother-in-law!"

"Then why come looking for Mrs. Austin?" Anna flashed at him.

He grinned. "Why not? I saw signs of activity as I was going past, and curiosity got the better of me."

"And now that curiosity is satisfied?" she asked mildly.

"Oh, but it isn't!" he protested. "Every now and again I do my duty and come along and visit Piran and the boy, but nobody could sat that the Trethowyn house is other than gloomy and full of recriminations on us all! To find anything as lovely as yourself makes it all worth while!"

Anna sat down on the settle, amused by his beautiful looks and his honeyed tongue. "Why do you keep coming?" she smiled at him.

"It's a two-way arrangement. Piran had very strong feelings about my sister and I like to keep them alive –"

"But that isn't kind!" Anna protested.

Michael Vaynor raised his eyebrows. When the light hit his eyes, she could see how blue they were. It was a well-practised gesture, she felt, but it was no less effective for that. He was the most winning individual she had met for a long, long time.

"The Vaynors aren't kind people," he observed as if he were talking abut some distant acquaintances. "Piran was a fool to get involved."

"But I thought your sister was dead," Anna said.

He nodded, still smiling. "She is. She was killed in a crash while she was running away from Piran. That's when the boy was injured."

Anna bit her lip. "Poor Piran," she said softly.

"Poor Caroline!" her brother countered. "She'd met a Frenchman while she was in Paris. If she were alive now, who can tell how happy she might have been?"

"And Peter?" she remarked dryly.

"The boy? Oh, he was devoted to his mother. She only took him with her because he cried all night when she told him she was going." He laughed briefly. "That stuck in Piran's gullet too, that the boy should prefer Caroline to him."

Anna felt her distaste at the conversation mounting within her. "I don't think we ought to be discussing it," she said frankly.

Michael Vaynor raised his eyebrows again. "No?" He sounded amused, as if he were laughing inwardly at some private joke. "Perhaps you're right," he admitted at length. "So what shall we talk about? You?"

"I don't think you would be interested," Anna said with dignity.

"That's what you think!" he retorted. He sat down carefully on the high-backed wooden chair and smiled at her, shaking his head from side to side. "I find you very interesting indeed! All Piran's affairs are of interest to me."

Anna was annoyed to feel herself blushing. "Indeed?"

He laughed to himself, enjoying the joke. "Do you find it an

28

unfortunate choice of word?" he asked. "You needn't. Piran's affairs are never romantic. In fact," he sighed, "they're strictly financial."

Anna stood up with resolution. "Mr. Vaynor," she began, "I think you'd do better to go up to the house. I've only just arrived and I want to get unpacked. So, if you'll excuse me –"

"I'll help!" he offered eagerly.

"I can manage by myself!" she told him flatly. "Some of my equipment is valuable. I *prefer* to look after it myself."

"Equipment?" He sounded quite bewildered. "Equipment for what?"

"I'm a lapidarist," Anna explained. She let the word roll from her tongue, enjoying the knowledge that he was no wiser than he had been. There was something about Michael Vaynor that left a bad taste in her mouth, despite his good looks and his confidence in his own peculiar brand of charm.

"Oh," he said. He didn't ask her to enlighten him as to what a lapidarist did, she noticed. "Is the stuff in those suitcases?" he asked her. He stood up and tried to lift one of the cases, pretending to find it heavier than it actually was. "What have you got here? The Crown Jewels?"

"Something like that," she agreed. She wished urgently that he would go.

"I must take a peek!" he taunted her. He made a quick attempt to open one of the suitcases. "Here, where's the key?"

"Mr. Vaynor –"

He looked up and grinned at her, his golden eyelashes curling against his cheek. "You're as stuffy as any Trethowyn!" he accused her. "Don't you know that nice girls don't tease strange men?"

"Mr. Vaynor, please go," Anna said quietly.

"Not till I've seen what you're hiding!" he laughed up at her. "Give me the key!"

Anna clenched her teeth, disliking him more than ever. She wondered if his sister had been like him; beautiful, golden and grasping. She thought it was only too likely, and her sympathy for Piran increased.

She knew that Michael Vaynor would try to take the key from her by force. She knew it as surely as she stood there, facing him, waiting for the smile to fade on his face as he realized that she was not going to hand it over.

When he came towards her, she shivered slightly, but she did not draw back. "Where do you keep it hidden?" he whispered. "In your handbag?"

"Mr. Vaynor –"

"I believe you're enjoying yourself," he remarked casually. "You're *much* too good for Piran!"

What he might have done to get the key from her, Anna never discovered. He put one hand on her shoulder and pulled her towards him, but she escaped his grasp easily enough. She took a step backwards, almost hitting her head on the hearth behind her. But Michael Vaynor was less fortunate. Neither of them had heard Piran come up the path. What they did hear was a yell of fury, followed by a swift blow that made Michael sit down quickly.

"Get out!" his brother-in-law ordered him.

Michael blinked at him. "I'm not doing any harm!" he said defensively.

"Get out!" Piran repeated. "Peter is waiting for you up at the house."

Both he and Anna watched in silence as Michael stooped low enough to get through the door. "I'll be back!" he announced with mock bravado. "I'll be back!"

Anna shivered again. She looked at Piran, her eyes wide with fear. "Thank you," she said with feeling.

Piran's glance took in her frightened face and the locked

30

suitcases on the floor. "Did he hurt you?" he asked briefly.

She shook her head. Without a word she took the keys out of her pocket and began to open the suitcases. Her hand trembled as she did so and she hoped that Piran hadn't noticed, but it seemed he had. He followed her movements with a grim expression on his face.

"It didn't take you two long to get together, did it?" he said with contempt.

Anna blushed. "Does he come often?" she countered.

Piran stared at her through angry eyes. "I'm sorry if I interrupted anything," he said stiffly.

"But you didn't!" she protested, almost in tears.

He gave her a lop-sided grin. "You forget," he said wryly, "that I know all about the Vaynor charm. I wouldn't be so sympathetic if I didn't!" he added bitterly.

It was her turn to be angry. "Charm!" she repeated scornfully. "He has as much charm as – as a scorpion! And he's a great deal more obvious!"

Piran's anger turned to surprise. She had the feeling that it was the first time he had seen her, really seen her as a person.

"Do you think so?" he asked, intrigued.

"Yes, I do," she said. She almost added that she hoped that Michael's sister had been a little less like him, but it wasn't a remark that she thought Piran would appreciate, so she kept it to herself.

"He's good for the boy," Piran sighed. "They understand one another."

Anna reminded herself that it was none of her business. She went on unpacking her things with slow deliberate movements. Most of the stuff she had with her was for her work. There was an electric polisher and the various bits and pieces that she used to shape and polish the different stones; she had a tumble polisher as well, into which she tipped the pebbles she

31

found and churned them round for them to polish one another, knocking off the dull outer coating that formed round the stone, to reveal the more colourful interior, sometimes streaked with various minerals, sometimes with a vein of a completely different kind of stone, making it interesting and, perhaps, unique. Then there were the different cloths, the heavy pieces of lead with which she rubbed certain marbles, rouge for the final touches, oils and varnishes, and quite a lot of silver out of which she fashioned her own settings for the rarer semi-precious gems that came her way.

All these she set up on the floor, carefully checking them in her mind to make sure that she had everything with her. There was little enough furniture in the room to get in her way and she thought that all she would need to get for herself was an old work-bench, or maybe one of those old-fashioned kitchen tables, too big for most modern houses, that were both sturdy and easy to keep clean.

"I came to tell you that Ellen will be bringing you some pots and pans from the kitchen. I don't think the old lady did much cooking. May I take a look and see what's there?"

Anna looked up and found Piran's eyes studying her thoughtfully.

"Yes, do," she said vaguely.

"You know," he remarked. "I think I had you wrong. You take all this stuff pretty seriously, don't you?"

She laughed, pushing the hair back out of her eyes. "Why shouldn't I?" she asked him.

He shrugged. "I don't know."

But she thought he did; she thought that his wife had probably been as superficial as her brother and that he judged all women to be the same.

"Won't Ellen be waiting for news of the pots and pans?" she reminded him gently.

The corners of his mouth tilted into a grin. "I'll tell her to bring you one of everything," he offered. He went over to the door and peered into the cooking area beyond. "There's nothing much here anyway – and what there is looks as thought it could be chucked out. Ugh! The frying pan can go for a start!" He looked at her over his shoulder. "What are you laughing at?"

She joined him in the doorway. "There's nothing wrong with the frying pan! All it wants is cleaning. I'll borrow a couple of wire-wool pads and do them myself." She tested one of the saucepans for weight and cleanliness. "They're nice and heavy anyway."

"Is that an advantage?"

She shook her head at him. "*I* think so," she said.

"I'll send Ellen over anyway," he promised. "I expect Michael will be taking the boy out somewhere, so she won't have much else to do."

Anna sniffed. She reminded herself again that it was none of her business how Peter spent his time. "Thank you very much," she said aloud.

But it was some time before Ellen came. Anna had finished unpacking her things and was engaged in putting her clothes away in the bedroom. The bedroom delighted in a quite different way from the ancient hearth in the other room. It was small and cramped, yet it contained all she needed; a bed, a well-scrubbed cupboard and a chest of drawers; but out of it, one could step down into a cool, dry cellar, called locally, a *fougou*, where once some fishwife had stored and salted down the vast catches of pilchards that had once fed most of Cornwall, but which had now apparently left the Cornish coasts for ever. It would make the ideal store-room for her pebbles and pieces of amethyst, coloured glass, quartz, jasper, serpentine, and anything else she could find.

She was still looking at the cellar when Ellen came in search of her.

"So you met Mr. Vaynor," she said brusquely, looking down at where Anna was standing.

"Yes, I did. He came here looking for Mrs. Austin."

"Maybe he did," Ellen conceded grudgingly. "She had a kindness for him from when he was a boy."

"Then he was brought up round here?" Anna said, surprised.

"Both he and his sister," Ellen agreed roughly. "Mr. Piran wants me to set the place straight for you. I'll clean the place through while you take your list to the shops. Maybe Mr. Vaynor will give you a lift," she added.

"I think not," Anna replied with decision. "Isn't there a bus into Penzance?"

Ellen's shoulders shook with silent laughter. "It goes every half hour. Tell me what you want to buy and I'll tell you the shops to go to."

Anna agreed and began to make out a list of the things she thought she would need. It all took longer than she would have believed possible, for Ellen had strong ideas on always buying the very best. "Don't you be put off, my dear. And don't you buy your cream and butter from anyone else. You go up the Arcade. You'll find the best there!"

Anna scribbled the various directions on to the edge of her list. "I hope I find half these places!" she commented ruefully.

Ellen's eyes lit up with sudden enthusiasm. "I could come with you," she suggested.

Anna hadn't the heart to refuse her. "All right," she said. "We can finish off here when we get back."

If she had had any idea of what it meant to take Ellen shopping, she never would have done it. Ellen knew the whole of

Penzance like the back of her hand. In every shop, she would exchange a cheerful greeting with someone who was evidently an intimate acquaintance of long standing. While she talked, exchanging the latest gossip of the day, Anna stood, first on one foot and then on the other, wondering how soon it would be before the inevitable exclamation: "So you've taken Chyanbara! It'll make a change for the poor boy, he has few enough people to talk to. Did Mr. Trethowyn bring you down the line from London?"

Anna was grateful for Ellen's invariable response. "Not he! It was the boy who let her the cabin."

"Do you know everyone in Penzance?" she asked Ellen as they hurried down the hill to the bus station, just beside the railway terminus.

"I'd not say everyone," Ellen said conservatively. "But I've lived about here all my life. I was married here, and buried my husband here. It was then that I went to work for the Trethowyns."

"Was that a long time ago?" Anna asked.

"Just the three years," Ellen responded. Anna wondered if she could ask her if Peter had been in a wheelchair for all that time, but Ellen took a deep breath and went on of her own accord. "I went to work for the Trethowyns the day after the accident. Mr. Piran himself asked me to live up at the house because his wife was away so much. He never knew, poor man, that that would be the very night –"

"But Peter was with his mother?" Anna asked.

Ellen sighed. "She couldn't bear him to be unhappy, poor mite. She went in to say good-bye to him, but the boy cried so she said he could go with her. In the morning it was all in the papers what had happened. The boy was the only one of the three of them to be alive. Mr. Piran went straight to London to get him, but the boy only wanted his mother –"

"But that's dreadful!" Anna exclaimed.

Ellen nodded sternly. "And she no better than she should be! But Mr. Piran never heeded that the boy was lonely. He was bitter from the hurt to his pride having his wife's affair in all the papers. He had no time for the boy."

Anna mounted the bus ahead of her companion. "Does Mr. Vaynor visit the house often?" she asked.

Ellen pursed up her lips in disapproval. "A sight too often, if you ask me! But there, Mr. Piran won't hear of showing him the door. The boy likes him, and that's enough for Mr. Piran."

Anna hesitated. "Is he – is he very like his sister?"

"They were as like as two peas in a pod to look at, but Mrs. Trethowyn hated anyone to be hurt or unhappy. I wouldn't say the same for Mr. Vaynor!" Ellen added with dislike. "He doesn't mind causing pain to anyone!"

When they got out of the bus, they shared the bags of shopping out between them, making sure that nothing was pressing down on the strawberries, the cream, or the eggs, then they walked up the hill in companionable silence, eager to get on with what they planned to do to the cottage.

"Why don't you stay and have lunch with me?" Anna suggested impulsively as they reached the fuchsia hedge that separated her little garden from that of the big house.

Ellen was flattered by the idea. She helped Anna stow away the provisions they had bought and then set to with a will to make the small cabin habitable. Between them, they scrubbed the floors, polished the copper, and cleaned the cooking equipment until it shone in the dim light that was all the rear windows permitted to enter the thick cob wall.

When they had finished, they were both exhausted, but the whole place was as clean as a new pin. Anna could have been living there for years, her equipment looked so settled in the

36

sparsely furnished living-room, the lumps of stone waiting for her to transform them into her particular kind of jewellery.

"It looks very nice!" Ellen declared in triumph.

Anna looked about her with appreciation. "It does, doesn't it?" she agreed. "Though I never would have managed without your help!"

Elen looked gratified. "I'll be off, up to the house, to see if the boy is back yet," she said, shying away from Anna's gratitude. "You have everything you need now?"

Anna walked with her to the fuchsia hedge and watched her cross the fine lawn under the trees and disappear into the house through the french windows. Then she turned and went back into the cottage. She hadn't thought it possible that anyone could be as happy as she was at that moment. The pride of possession burgeoned within her and she laughed aloud at her own satisfaction in the place she had come to. She had come to Cornwall, the place of her mother's descent and her own dreams. And even the best of those dreams, she decided, were but a shadow of the reality. For the first time in her adult life she felt at home.

CHAPTER THREE

ANNA heard Peter's chair long before he reached her door. She looked up and saw him in the doorway, staring at her, his tousled black hair even more awry than she had seen it the day before.

"Did you sleep well?" he asked politely.

"Very!" She got up from behind the table where she had been working. "Would you like some coffee?"

Peter looked pleased. "I'm not interrupting you or anything? The thing is, I hadn't anything much to do —"

"That's all right," Anna said easily. "I'll get the coffee. I shan't be a minute."

She could see the boy from the doorway and watched him as he wheeled himself closer to the table and began to look at the tumbler-polished pebbles she had left lying on the table.

"Do you know what they all are?" she asked him.

He nodded. "Sure. You've got some quite nice bits here, haven't you? I particularly like this piece of quartz-veined slate. What are you going to do with it?"

"Turn it into a pendant, I think."

Peter smiled slowly, but the smile never reached his eyes. "Is that what you do with all of them?"

"Mostly. The smaller ones I make into bracelets and things like that." She dropped some instant coffee into the bottom of two mugs and poured boiling water into them, topping the lot with the cream off the top of the milk. "Here you are!" she said, as she put his mug down on the table beside him.

"I have quite a good collection of pebbles," he volunteered cautiously. "I've got some very pretty pieces of serpentine. I'll show you, if you like?"

Anna found it easy to be enthusiastic about that. "I long to go and get some pieces for myself," she said.

"There are buses that go," he told her indifferently. He braced himself against the arm of his chair to reach out for a stone that was on the other side of the table. "Of course," he added, "I can't go in a bus easily."

"No," she said.

"We have a car. Piran took the front seat out for me." He turned and looked at her. "If you take me with you, we could go in that."

Anna sipped at her coffee. It was very hot and she had made it rather too strong for her own taste. "Would your father like that?" she asked him.

"Sure. Why not? He'll be glad to have me out from under his feet!"

"We'll have to ask him," she warned him.

His face took on a stormy look. "If you like," he said.

She hesitated, wondering how to ask her question. "Peter," she said at last. "Don't you do any schooling?"

He shrugged. "When I feel like it."

"But you don't go to school?"

His lips twisted bitterly. "No," he said abruptly. "I do a so-called correspondence course. It will be different when I get out of this chair, but that will be years away – or never! – and Piran likes to rub it in."

"Rub what in?" Anna exclaimed, shocked.

"How Mother died," he said abruptly. "And how *innocent* he was! He drove her to it!"

Anna swallowed. "Are you sure?" she said carefully.

He nodded. "Mike told me. Who could stick it here?" he added sourly. "I only do because I have to."

Anna forced herself to laugh. "Good heavens!" she said.

39

"You must be very hard to please! I've never seen a lovelier house than yours —"

"But Cornwall is miles away from London!"

"Well, I've lived in London all my life," Anna assured him, "and I don't miss it one bit!"

"Mike prefers London," he said doggedly.

"Then why doesn't he live there?" Anna asked reasonably.

Peter stared at her for a long moment. "I don't know," he said slowly.

"Quite," Anna said with decision. "Now, tell me about these other pebbles. Where's the best place to go looking for them?"

By the time Peter had told her of the best locations for each kind of stone, the sulky look had quite left his face. He knew a great deal about the subject, especially about the local gemstones — amethyst, citrine, chalcedony, jasper, bloodstone or heliotrope, carnelian, opal, agate and onyx; he knew them all and exactly where they were to be found.

"I spend hours on the beaches looking for them," he confessed. "Anywhere I can go in my chair. It's rather frustrating when I can't get about, but I can show you where to go. May I? I mean, I'd like to, if you won't find me in the way?"

She was touched by his sudden humility. "Like it! I can think of nothing nicer!"

Peter grinned at her, and this time the smile did reach his eyes. "It will be the greatest fun!" he said with satisfaction.

When Peter had wheeled himself back across the lawn to his own house, Anna thought she would try and find Piran to ask him herself if he would mind Peter going with her when she went searching for the raw materials of her work. She found Ellen in the garden, picking some roses for the house.

"He'll be at the Meadhouse," she said. "You'll find it in the village."

"*Mead?*" Anna repeated. "Do they still make it?"

Ellen shook her head at her. "They do. It's quite an industry hereabouts. The Trethowyns have been making mead ever since the end of the war. They've made a fine thing out of it! Have you never had any?"

"Never!" said Anna.

"Then you'd best go down to the Meadhouse and try some," Ellen suggested slyly. "Mr. Piran can serve you himself."

The Meadhouse was quite obvious when Anna came into the village. She went through the churchyard, where the flame trees were in flower, and marvelled that such exotic plants should grow anywhere in England. On the other side of the small square beyond the church was the Meadhouse. On either side were the small granite terraced houses with their slate roofs that are so common locally, most of them with window-boxes, or even with purple campanula growing in the cracks in the pointing. The Meadhouse, on the contrary, had recently received a bright coat of pink wash, with a glossy black door and accessories. Outside the door stood a couple of tubs packed full of plants of every hue that added to the gaiety. On closer inspection, she saw that the building was extremely old, perhaps even old enough to have belonged to the early Norman period. There was a stream too that ran through the small garden and a weeping willow that hung over the water, its trailing branches dancing over the water in the light breeze.

Anna went up the few, uneven steps that led to the entrance and pushed open the door which led, not as she had expected into the house, but into a paved courtyard. A tall girl dressed in a trouser suit came out into the courtyard at exactly the same moment.

"I'm afraid we're not open," she said languidly.

"I wondered if Mr. Trethowyn was here?" Anna said weakly. There was something about the other girl that over-

41

awed her. She thought she had never seen anyone so perfectly groomed. She had a large, rather flat face and eyes that were probably short-sighted and which protruded out of pale lids. She looked rather like a Dutch painting, but her appearance was so immaculate that her lack of beauty became an asset in itself.

"Mr. Trethowyn? Is he expecting you?" She sounded slightly surprised, as if she thought she knew all about Piran's affairs.

"I don't think so," said Anna.

"Then?" The other girl looked towards the door and began to go back into the house.

"Then I want to see him," Anna said smoothly, refusing to be intimidated.

The girl smiled agreeably. "If it's urgent, perhaps I can help you?" she offered.

"It's kind of you," Anna said, "but I want to see Mr. Trethowyn personally."

The girl looked annoyed. Her pale eyes reflected her anger clearly. She shrugged her shoulders petulantly. "What name?" she snapped.

"Anna St. James."

The girl stopped short in her tracks. "I've heard about you," she said. "You're living in the cabin, aren't you? Peter gets his own way far too often, in my opinion!"

Anna raised her brows in polite enquiry. The girl gave a short, sharp laugh.

"You didn't suppose Piran wanted you there, did you?" she said flatly. "I don't suppose Peter would have suggested it if he hadn't known that Piran was going to offer it to me. It all adds fuel to the fire of their dislike for one another!"

Anna said nothing. She wondered who the girl was. She looked about her and saw a group of painted tables and chairs in one corner of the paved courtyard. She wandered over towards them and sat down on the nearest chair.

"Is Mr. Trethowyn here?" she asked politely.

The other girl shrugged and went back into the house. She came back a few seconds later and began setting out the tables in a great flurry, pretending to ignore the fact that Anna was still there.

It was quite a long time before Piran came out. He came across to Anna immediately, patently surprised to see her sitting there.

"I did give you a call," the other girl said defensively. "She wants to see you."

Piran smiled at Anna. "Do you?" he asked her with interest.

"It's about Peter," she said uncomfortably.

"Oh yes?" He sounded only vaguely interested. "By the way, Wendy Morris is my assistant here. Wendy, come and meet Peter's new tenant, Anna St. James."

The two girls' hands touched briefly. Anna was conscious of the limp displeasure of the other girl and hoped that it wasn't as obvious to Piran.

"Do you make the mead here?" she asked, intrigued.

"Yes," Piran answered her. "Do you want to see?"

She nodded. "What is it made from? Ale and honey?"

"Mostly honey," he said.

"Why don't you try some?" Wendy suggested briefly. "I'll get you a glass." She sounded suddenly more friendly than she had before.

As soon as she had gone, Anna turned impulsively to Piran. "About Peter," she began with a rush.

Piran frowned slightly. "Yes?"

Anna took a deep breath. "Does it annoy you to talk about your son?" she asked him, put out by his manner.

Piran gave her a surprised look. "Good heavens, no! Do I

43

give that impression?"

She nodded. "Sometimes. Anyway, he would like to come with me when I go looking for pebbles. I thought I'd better ask you first. Have you any objection?"

He stood for a long moment, looking her straight in the face. She bore his scrutiny bravely, thinking with some amusement that he would certainly know her again.

"Have you?" she prompted him.

"Me? No." He laughed briefly. "Peter is old enough to make up his own mind who he wants to go out with. I don't keep him in leading reins, you know."

Her eyes dropped. She was rather embarrassed by his searching eyes now. Enough was enough, she thought.

"Perhaps you should mind more," she said gently.

"What do you mean by that?"

She looked up, meeting his eyes firmly. "Thirteen is not very old."

Piran shrugged. "He wouldn't listen to me anyway," he excused himself. "I keep an eye on him in my own way, but I try not to antagonise him by making it too obvious." He made a gesture with his hands. "I do try to learn by my mistakes," he said.

Anna hesitated. "I suppose it isn't any of my business –" she began.

"No, it isn't," he cut her off sharply.

Anna looked down at the floor in a meek gesture she was far from feeling. "Then I take it that you have no objection to his coming with me?" she asked carefully.

"None at all," he said. "He'll show you where the car is. I suppose you can drive?" he added as an afterthought.

"Oh yes," she assured him. "But I think I'll find my own transport –"

"Rubbish! The boy is used to travelling in the same car. It

takes his chair without any difficulty. He finds it more comfortable than anything else."

Anna might have argued the point, for she frankly preferred to be independent of the Trethowyns. She thought she was sufficiently involved with them already, without putting herself any further in their debt. But there was no time for her to continue the conversation. As far as Piran Trethowyn was concerned, it was all settled.

Wendy Morris brought out three small glasses and a bottle of mead, tall and with steeply sloping shoulders rather like a bottle of hock. She put the glasses down on the table and filled them each in turn.

"You might not like it," she warned Anna. "Some people don't. You can get it a lot sweeter than this, but we prefer this recipe."

Anna took a sip. She was afraid that she would find it too sweet, but it wasn't. It tasted rather like sherry, only the pungent flavour of honey was left on her tongue to remind her of the main ingredient of this ancient drink.

"Do you like it?" Piran asked her, smiling.

"It's delicious!" she exclaimed.

He was amused by her enthusiasm. "We think so," he said. "It's catching on well now with the tourist industry. I like to think it's a very Cornish thing!"

"Made with Cornish hands!" Anna added dryly.

"Why not?" he said simply. "We thought of it!"

She laughed and, after a minute, he laughed with her. Wendy tossed her drink down with a sigh of pleasure and smiled at them both.

"You have to admit," she said earnestly, "that we make a very pleasant drink. It's the best!" She linked arms with Piran with a possessive air. "We've built up the whole place between us! Trethowyn and Morris!"

45

"The first Morris was your father," Piran reminded her gravely. He liked to get his facts straight in exactly the same was as Peter did.

"That was only when the idea was first mooted," Wendy retorted crossly. "He went to London almost immediately and *I* went on with it."

Anna clicked her tongue, unable to resist the temptation. "He went to *London*? To take work away from the Londoners?" she asked gravely.

Piran's eyes flashed dangerously. "His wasn't that kind of job!" he retorted. His anger died as quickly as it had risen. "Come inside and see what we're doing to it. We're near enough to Penzance here for people to walk out as far as Penwith in the evening. This year we're doing a lot of local advertising in the hotels and so on."

He made a very good guide. He pointed out the features of the old building they had reclaimed for their purpose. It had once belonged to a seed merchant and, in some of the less used corners, it still smelt of corn and birdseed and cattle-cake. The cellars where they made the mead were scrupulously clean, however, with the mead neatly stacked in new-looking metal kegs and a few of the older wooden variety. Beside the kegs, in another part of the cellars, were samples of the various containers into which they poured the golden liquid to sell it. There were bottles, stone jars, and ornamental glass, made in half a dozen different shapes to appeal to every taste, for if some people had a fancy for a Cornish pisky, others quite definitely did not.

Anna studied the containers carefully. Before she had begun to work exclusively with jewellery she had made similar articles, some of which, she thought privately, were of a considerably higher quality than any of these. She said nothing, however, only she couldn't quite resist fingering some of the

46

prettier jars, testing them with her supple fingers for strength and examining how easy they were to fill and whether they poured out easily and well.

Piran watched her closely. "Well?" he asked.

She blushed, nearly dropping the jar she was holding. "I – I was just looking!"

"And what conclusions did you come to?" he pressed her.

It was Wendy who came to her rescue. "She doesn't know anything about it," she said bluntly. "You're embarrassing her."

But Piran brushed aside her protests. "Is that true?" he demanded of Anna.

"That you're embarrassing me? I suppose it is," she answered meekly.

"But you do know something about it?"

"Not much," she admitted. She glanced down at her watch. "I must be going," she went on hastily. "I hadn't realised how quickly the time has gone."

But Piran was not so easily put off. "I want to know what you think of that jar," he said stubbornly.

Wendy gave him a cross look. "It isn't even your department," she reminded him smugly. "I look after that side of things!"

"That doesn't mean we can't do with some fresh ideas," he said abruptly. "Well, Anna?"

"I don't know that I have any ideas," Anna dismissed his question. "I think some of these are very pretty –"

"And practical?" he insisted.

"It isn't always easy to turn out something both pretty and practical," she answered evasively, aware of Wendy's increasing resentment. "And I only came to ask if I can take Peter out with me."

Piran turned his back on her. "Do what you like!" he said

tartly. "I'll see you around."

"He's a bit moody," Wendy explained apologetically as she escorted Anna up the stairs from the cellar and out again into the sunlight. "He's been the same ever since his wife was killed. Have you heard about that?"

Anna nodded. "He still has Peter," she said gently.

Wendy looked at her incredulously. "But he doesn't *want* Peter! What he needs is a completely new marriage without any appendages to remind him of – of that other time. Besides," she added, "Peter prefers being with his Uncle Michael. I think it would be a very neat solution." She sounded so pleased with her own reasoning that Anna said nothing. Perhaps there was another side to Michael Vaynor that she hadn't seen, but she would have thought him a most unfortunate influence on any young boy.

"Does Mr. Vaynor want Peter?" Anna asked.

Wendy shrugged. "I should think so." Her eyes opened very wide. "His mother left him quite a lot of money," she added. "Piran won't touch a penny of it, but Michael would have to if he were to have the boy."

Anna was shocked. It occurred to her that the last thing she ought to be doing was to discuss the Trethowyns with anyone. She hardly knew them, and anyway it was none of her business. If she hoped that it wasn't any of Wendy's business either, that was quite by the way, and she had no right to object she knew. But never would she have thought that she would have been so interfering as to gossip about anyone she had only just met!

"Thank you for showing me round," she said with careful good manners.

Wendy smiled. "Any time," she said carelessly. "As a matter of fact I like to do the honours for Piran. It's awkward for a man on his own, don't you think? Not that his wife took much

48

interest when she was here!" Wendy smiled conspiratorially. "But that's between ourselves," she added. "He doesn't like people to hang round his neck!"

Anna was thoughtful as she walked back through the churchyard to her cottage. She found she was interested in the Trethowyns almost despite herself, but she had the uneasy feeling that she didn't understand them and that they might well hurt her in a way from which she would not easily recover. It was ridiculous to think such a thing, she kept telling herself, but the conviction wouldn't go away. It was still there to haunt her when she let herself into the cottage and stood idly playing with the polished stones on her work-table.

Peter must have been waiting for her, for she heard his chair crunching on the path outside and a second later he had wheeled himself into the room beside her.

"What did you think of our honeyed mead?" he asked her, rather sourly, she thought.

She smiled inattentively. "I liked it," she said.

He looked at her closely. "Really?"

"Yes, why not?"

To her surprise, he looked embarrassed. "Well – it's a real drink, of course, but it doesn't seem quite real, does it? Especially with Wendy floating round the place like some chatelaine out of the Middle Ages!"

Anna stifled a quick laugh. "Does she?" she said. "She seemed quite ordinary this morning."

"They weren't open," Peter answered dryly. "I say, you don't mind my coming over here to talk to you, do you?"

"No," Anna said easily.

The boy gave her a strained shy smile that went to her heart. "It's a bit lonely up at the house," he explained. "I get bored by myself."

"I asked your father if you could come out with me," she
49

told him.

"But there was no need for that! I told you it would be all right!" He laughed shortly. "I bet Wendy thought you were making a fuss about nothing! She would love me to go away so that she can have Piran to himself. I'd go too, if I thought Mike really wanted me."

Anna's heart caught at the loneliness in his voice. "I think your father needs you," she said gently. "He needs you more than anyone else."

Peter made a face at her. "Fairy stories!" he accused her. "I don't need anyone either! At least," he added uncomfortably, "I wouldn't if I could get out of this chair. But I'll do that one day, and then none of them will see me for dust!"

Anna refused to take his remarks seriously. "I'd miss you," she told him lightly, "but I have my work to keep me going!"

Peter laughed despite himself. "I wasn't talking about you, silly!"

Anna raised her eyebrows severely. "Silly?" she repeated. "Have you no respect?"

His eyes flashed with amusement. "You're good fun!" he exclaimed. "Can I help you make some of your jewellery?"

"If you like. But shouldn't you be doing your lessons?"

Peter shrugged his shoulders. "The lessons come once a month," he told her. "To tell you the truth, I've usually finished them in less than a week. So I have plenty of time for other things."

She wondered if it were true. She thought he was clever enough. He had an air of sharp, impatient intelligence that appealed to her, but it didn't always mean that when the time came he would pass his exams as easily as he expected. Perhaps, when she knew him better, she would offer to help him, but that time was not yet.

She smiled at him. "You won't think that I'm making use

of you?" she tested him. "I really could do with some help if you mean it. I have quite a few London contracts to fulfil and I'll be hard put to it to do it all by myself."

"All you've got to do is to tell me what to do," he said.

She offered him her hand in solemn agreement. "Here," she said, "I have a couple of books which will give you some idea. But the first thing to do is to get out and find some stones. I want to get some serpentine, and I want to go to some beach where there are some good pebbles –"

"Loe Bar," Peter said thoughtfully. "We could go there on the way back from the Lizard."

Anna wrinkled up her brow. "I don't think I've heard of it," she said.

"It's the very best!" he told her with enthusiasm. "It's formed by a whole bank of pebbles thrown up by the storms that come across Mount's Bay from time to time. It blocks up the outlet of the Cober river. It's beautiful! You have the sea on one side and a kind of lake made by the river on the other. I'd like to go there, if you think you can manage my chair," he added diffidently.

"Why not?" she said, catching his enthusiasm. "Shall we go now?"

He was plainly pleased. He set off at a tremendous pace across the garden towards the large double garage that held the car that had been modified to take his chair. The sulky look had completely gone from his dark face as he looked over his shoulder to hurry her along. But, at the corner of the house, he came to a complete stop and she watched his shoulders hunch and the pout come back to his mouth. With a quick sigh she hurried forward to his side, to see Piran standing by the garage door.

"We're going out," Peter informed his father belligerently.

Piran nodded. He said nothing, but he began to open the

51

garage doors. The hinges creaked with rust and he gave them a kick and smiled slightly as a cloud of red dust settled at his feet.

"You – you did say I could take him," Anna reminded him, annoyed with herself for being nervous of him.

He smiled openly at her, the sudden charm of which she was so conscious making her heart hammer within her

"I thought I'd come with you," he said. "That is, if you have no objection?"

Both she and Peter shook their heads. He got into the driving seat and eased the car out of the garage. He knew exactly what to do with Peter's chair, locking the brake firmly, and covering his son's legs with a flimsy rug.

"Do you care to drive?" he asked Anna, dangling the keys before her.

"Wouldn't you rather –?" she began.

"No, I wouldn't," he retorted. "I want to see if you can handle a car, or if like most females you allow the car to handle you!"

Anna took a firm hold of her temper and took the keys from him with a hand that didn't even tremble. It was strange, she thought, that being with him was just like being on a scenic railway. He was charming and completely hateful by turns, and she didn't know which was worse. Only the sight of Peter's chair reminded her that he had cause to see for himself if she could drive before he trusted her with his son, kept her from making the angry retort that rose to her lips. Not this time, Piran Trethowyn, she thought, but one day he would go too far and she would enjoy doing battle with him. She hadn't the slightest doubt that she would be the victor.

CHAPTER FOUR

THERE was a mist hanging over Lizard Town. It blew in snatches across the streets and the square of rough grass behind the hotel where Piran suggested that they should park the car.

"I expect the boy will want to show you round the shanties," he drawled. "I think most of the men round here have put up with his questions for years. He knows them all."

"Aren't you coming?" Anna asked him. She felt an overwhelming sense of disappointment that he should sit in the car and wait for them when he ought to have been joining in, if only for Peter's sake.

"I'll walk down to the point," he answered languidly. He swung Peter's chair to the ground and helped the boy into it. "Okay?" he asked him.

"Okay," Peter agreed.

Piran didn't waste much time. He walked quickly away from them down an old farm track towards the sea. The mist shrouded him almost immediately, with the odd patch of sunlight suddenly revealing his progress again. Anna watched his departure in silence, but Peter paid no attention to his father at all. He tested the wheels of his chair in the grass, grunting with the effort of wheeling himself out into the road to where the shanties, filled with their serpentine wares to catch the tourists, lay waiting for the passer-by to come inside and buy.

Peter had his own ideas as to which were the best stalls. He was in high good humour because he reckoned that he really knew about the possibilities of this soapy, highly coloured granite and he was longing to show off his knowledge to Anna.

53

He led her first of all down a small side-street to where an old man was busy working, polishing a piece of the stone on an electrically driven leather belt. The old man nodded a dour greeting to the boy.

"Thought it was about time you were over," he said. "Haven't seen you for a week or so. It'll be the season soon and I'll have no time for you then!"

Peter grinned at him. "It's the season now!" he exclaimed.

"Ay, but it ain't like August, now is it?'

Peter shook his head. "I've brought a friend to see you," he said. "She makes jewellery and stuff out of pebbles – you know the sort of thing. I thought she might like to see the things you make."

The old man crinkled up his eyelids and peered at Anna through the mist. "You're welcome to take a look inside my shanty," he offered.

She accepted gratefully, taking stock of his tiny work-room, which was really no more than a badly-built wooden shed with a window at one side that had been turned into a kind of counter where he could display his goods and sell them to the customers as they passed by along the road. He had a great number of objects for sale, all of them fashioned out of serpentine. There were beautiful serpentine eggs, dark green or grey in colour, with splashes of blue and gold and pink; there were paper knives and fruit knives; lighthouses, paperweights, door handles, eggcups, and a whole lot of odd pieces of the rock, polished on one side only to reveal the fantastic colours that stained the basic green, blood-red and greys of the stone.

"How do you get it so smooth?" she asked him with admiration.

He grunted something into his beard, reaching down for a lump of lead. "Start with this," he muttered. "Give it a good rub. Polishing all the time on the leather. Rouge next and

54

more polishing. When it's done, I put on a good, clear varnish. Some of it is better than other bits. Look at this one!"

Anna took the piece of stone from him. It had been roughly shaped into a seagull in flight and the colours were indeed beautiful. Somehow the jagged edges of the stone had become the feathers of the bird and only the beak, the eyes and the almost hidden feet were polished. In other shops, she was sure that she would see much the same thing, reproduced many thousands of times, and yet this one example was in its way a work of art. He had caught the muscular sweep of the bird's wings, the set of its head, and the bright cruelty of its eyes.

"It looked like a bird," the old man told her simply. "It was there in the rock. I'm not selling that piece easily."

"I think it's terrific!" Peter enthused happily.

The old man was embarrassed. "Here's a piece for yourself," he said to Anna. He reached down into a sack and drew out a piece of untouched serpentine that had come straight from the quarry. "Are you going to turn out some bits yourself?"

"I was half thinking of seeing if I couldn't make some bottles out of serpentine. Would it be possible?"

"Depends on how handy you are," he grunted unanswerably.

"I have some quite good equipment," she assured him.

"Then you'd manage no doubt. You'd need to drill for the inside and polish it too, but if you have the tools it wouldn't be impossible." His bright blue eyes looked at her keenly. "Setting up in competition, are you?"

"Oh no!" she said hastily. "I don't think I'd attempt to make any of the sort of things you make. You see, I have my own market, mostly jewellery and that sort of thing. I have to fulfil those contracts before I do anything else."

"Ah!" he said knowledgeably. "Contracts! Them legal things isn't practical in our shanties. We just make things in the winter and sell them in the summer. Ain't much to it, but it serves as a living. But they bottles you have in mind is a good idea, just so long as you make them right, and no reason why you shouldn't either!" He patted Peter awkwardly on the shoulder. "As for you, my handsome, you show her the quarry and get her some good stone – nothing crumbly – no rubbish, mind you!"

"I'll see to it," Peter nodded solemnly. "Come on," he said to Anna, "Piran will be waiting."

They shook hands with the old man and then made a quick tour of the other shanties in the town. There were one or two that were more sophisticated than the old man's, though they seemed to Anna to sell exactly the same things, but Peter passed them all by with no more than a wave of the hand.

"He's the only artist amongst them!" he explained contemptuously.

Anna paused by one of the windows. "I don't know," she said slowly. "Some of these things are very pretty."

Peter frowned at her. "Pretty baubles!" he snorted.

"They're very pretty baubles!" she insisted. "Why not? If they give pleasure?"

Peter thumped his closed fists on the side of his chair. "There's a difference," he maintained. "The old man's bird is a work of art. These are all the same. Nice souvenirs, but they're nothing more than that."

"They're not trying to be," Anna said stubbornly.

He gave her a mischievous look. "Is that what you plan that your bottles should be?" he asked lightly.

Anna blushed. The bottles were an idea she preferred to keep to herself. "They might be too difficult to make," she said gruffly.

Peter balanced his chair at the top of a slope and glided smoothly down to the bottom. "Oh, my!" he exclaimed over his shoulder. "Wendy is going to love you!"

Anna's blush deepened. "I didn't say they were going to hold mead!" she objected. "I might be making them for perfume – anything!"

"Huh!" said Peter.

"Do you think you could shove me down to the point?" Peter asked. His voice sounded edgy as it always did when he was reminded of his handicap. "It's rather a long way."

"I'd like to," Anna said with decision. "I didn't offer because you manage everything so well for yourself, but I'd always like to help if I can."

Peter was silent for a minute and she was afraid she had offended him. "At least you don't make a meal of it." he said grudgingly.

"I should hope not!" Anna deliberately sounded shocked.

"I've known people with much worse things! Besides, you won't be in a chair for ever! That would be much worse!"

"I sometimes wonder about that," said Peter. "Nobody says anything much, but surely I ought to be doing exercises or something if I'm going to walk again?"

"Have you asked anyone?" Anna suggested.

"No. I don't like to talk about it normally," he admitted.

"Well, if you do, I'll help you with anything you have to do," she said in the same matter-of-fact tones.

He looked over his shoulder at her, his dark eyes wide and suspicious. "I could probably manage by myself," he said.

"It's more fun with somebody else, though," Anna put in. She was relieved when he didn't argue the matter any further. He hadn't had much of a time, she thought, since his mother had died, but it wouldn't do to make one's sympathy for him too obvious. She gave the chair a shove over some loose stones and wondered why the Trethowyns had to be such touchy people.

Piran Trethowyn was sitting on the grass, staring out to sea across the southernmost part of England. The mauve-pink thrift surrounded him in drifts of colour and the bright green of the grass was lit up as the sun struggled through the sea mist and finally banished it completely from the point. Piran stood up as they approached.

"Well?" he said to his son.

Peter scowled at him. "You should have come back," he said crossly. "My chair is too heavy for Anna to push."

Piran refused to be drawn. "Has she been complaining?" he asked lightly.

"Of course not!" Anna disclaimed quickly. "It was worth all the cow-pats to see the view from here! Besides," she added with a touch of mischief, "you can push him back!"

"Yes, he can!" Peter agreed with satisfaction.

Anna took in the hurt look on Piran's face and changed the subject. "What's that rather pretty cove down there? I caught a glimpse of it as we came past a gate?"

"That's Kynance," Peter answered her before his father could. "Why don't you both take a look at it?"

"We don't want to leave you on your own," Piran told him.

The boy looked up at him. "That for a yarn! I *prefer* being on my own, as you very well know!"

Piran ignored him. "If you walk along there," he told Anna, pointing out the path, "you can see the Lizard lighthouse. They're quite pleased to have visitors there."

But Anna shook her head. "I'm going to the edge of the point," she announced. She smiled suddenly. "In a way, it's more romantic than Land's End, don't you think?" She didn't wait for an answer, but ran down the slope to where the cliff curved upwards again, jutting out into a point that looked no more significant than half a dozen others along the coast, but which happened to be the one that probed furthest south of them all.

When she stood on the point itself, she became nervous of the height and wondered if the cliffs ever gave way. Slowly, she eased herself on to her hands and knees and peered downwards at the dark blue sea below and the folds of golden granite, shaped to fantastic shapes by the constant action of the sea. The mist had been chased away entirely and the sun brought out the brilliance of the green and gold. High above her the sea birds danced their stately aerial ballets, screeching to one another with their ugly voices. Below, with only its black head showing in the water, a shag dived for fish and rose again, shaking itself free of an iridescent cloud of water, and dived again.

Piran came after her and threw himself down beside her, lighting a cigarette.

"The boy is in a quarrelsome mood," he remarked.

Anna played with a single blade of grass, marvelling at how neatly it folded into the stalk that held it. "Do you think so?"

"I'm thinking of sending him away," Piran went on abruptly. "He needs people of his own age to talk to."

"Where would you send him?" Anna asked, her spirits sinking.

Piran shrugged. "His uncle wants to have him live with him in London." Anna rolled over, supporting herself on one elbow so that she could see him better. "Michael Vaynor?" she said.

"I have no right to dislike him as much as I do," Piran admitted slowly. "He means well with the boy."

Anna strove to keep a still tongue in her face. "Does he?" she asked ironically. "I should think again, Mr. Trethowyn."

Piran's face darkened with anger. "You didn't appear to dislike him much yourself!" he accused her unjustly. "Perhaps you were already missing your gay life in London?"

She forced a laugh. "What gay life?" she said.

He gave her a lopsided grin which held no kindness at all. "A pretty girl like you expects a good time," he grunted. "I have reason to know!"

She was startled. "Oh?" she said blankly. Perhaps he did know, she thought uneasily, if other girls had found him as attractive as she did. Or perhaps it was his wife that had put the idea in his head? She didn't know. All she did know was that she was afraid, as much of herself as of him.

"But we're not above having a little of your kind of life in Cornwall!" His mouth curled contemptuously.

Anna sat up very straight. "*My* kind of life?" she repeated.

"Why not?" Piran went on bitterly. "I expect I'd enjoy it as much as any other man!"

"Would you?" she said gently.

"Would you?" he countered.

It wasn't in Anna's nature to lie. She wondered if he had any idea of how attractive he was to her. *Keep it light,* she told herself breathlessly. *Whatever you do, keep it light!*

'I really couldn't say," she managed. "I've never experienced –" Her voice died away into silence.

Piran stubbed out his cigarette and rose to his feet with deliberation. "Never?" he said brutally. He bent over her, putting a hand beneath her elbows and lifting her almost bodily to her feet. "I wish I could believe you!"

Anna swallowed. "You can," she said steadily. She ought to be frightened of him, she knew, but she was not. Despite his strength, and his anger, and even the dislike that was clearly written on his face, she still wasn't afraid of him. He's going to kiss me, she thought, and waited for the panic that such an idea should have had. But there was none. All she felt was an exultant leap within her as his lips met hers. I must be mad, she told herself. Mad, mad, mad! But it was a joyous madness. The gulls screeched and the thrift became a pink blur.

The gentle pounding of the sea below became the drumming of her own blood. He kissed her quite gently at first, and then it wasn't gentle at all, and she knew that she was kissing him back. It was quite different from any of the light kisses she had ever exchanged with a man before.

"I thought as much!" Piran said with disgust.

"I – I –" Anna stammered.

"You do it very well," he congratulated her smoothly. "Shall we go back to Peter?"

She nodded bleakly. So that was all there was to it. She felt a tight, constricted anger that something so beautiful should have been offered to her by way of an insult. Why, oh, why did she have to fall for such a man? It wasn't *fair*! And yet who cared about fairness? She would, she knew, have given years of her life to do no more than to wipe away the lines of bitterness on his face. She felt more helpless than she had ever done.

"At least," Piran goaded her, "we needn't go on pretending. Women are all the same! All of you like to have something going on the side!"

"Isn't that somewhat sweeping?" Anna protested, annoyed that her voice should tremble so perilously.

He looked at her with that same hateful smile. "Are you going to pretend you didn't enjoy it?" he demanded arrogantly.

She shook her head. "No."

"I suppose I should have known you were welcoming Michael too!"

She faced him squarely. "If you want to know, I dislike your brother-in-law very much!" she told him flatly. "Nor would I trust him with anyone, let alone a son of mine! Not that it's any business of mine," she added forlornly.

"No, it isn't," he agreed unpleasantly.

61

Anna was dismayed to feel the tears stinging at the back of her eyes. How much happier she had been when she had felt nothing but an uncomplicated hatred for the man beside her — if she ever had! If she were honest, she thought, most of the humiliation she had felt at that first meeting had been because he had been so attractive to her! No, she had never really hated him, and now she knew that she didn't hate him at all. Far from it! If she could have gained his respect, she might have been able to bear it. But then she had never had his respect. No woman had had that since his wife had taken his feelings for her and broken them into tiny pieces by killing herself in a car crash. And, if there had been any danger of his forgetting, there was Peter to remind him of it every day, a cripple in a wheelchair, the one miserable result of the whole affair. And Wendy —! Now what on earth had made her think of her?

"Oh, lord!" said Piran. "Are you going to cry?"

"No!" she sniffed indignantly.

Somehow this obvious untruth made him smile. "My dear girl —"

"I am *not* your dear girl!"

"No, of course not," he agreed. "I didn't mean to be patronising. But I think you'd better dry your eyes before Peter sees you. He'd probably jump to the conclusion that I'd been beating you!"

"You might just as well have done!" she told him. But she obediently wiped her eyes and tried to smile at him.

He looked puzzled. "But you said you liked it well enough?"

"That's not the point!" she burst out, stamping her foot.

"No?" He laughed gently and no longer unkindly. "One day you must tell me what the point is!" he teased her.

She sighed. How could she ever explain that what should have been one of the loveliest experiences of her life had been

62

tarnished, cheapened, and made thoroughly undesirable? There had never been anyone before that she had wanted to kiss, and now when every fibre of her being welcomed this strange, moody man she barely knew, he had shown pretty clearly just what he thought of her, and the knowledge was unbearable.

Anna made a thing of looking at Kynance Cove from the gateway as they walked back to Lizard Town. She thought it would distract Peter's dark eyes from staring at her face and seeing things that she would rather he didn't see. But it was too much to hope that he had been looking the other way when his father had kissed her. He hadn't.

"Wendy will be after you!" he whispered to her as she struggled to get the rug over his knees away from the spokes of the wheels.

"You should mind your own business," she told him harshly.

He laughed at her. "Much you care! I'm surprised at you, Anna St. James!"

"It didn't mean anything," she said.

"Not to Piran either?" She thought he sounded faintly wistful, as if he were jealous of his father even if he wouldn't admit it. It was an encouraging sign, if one day they were to be friends.

"It meant less than nothing to him!" she answered him. She was dismayed at the bitterness in her voice, but the boy appeared to notice nothing.

"My mother always kissed everyone all round," he said suddenly. "It was Piran then who always got cross. Now he seems quite good at kissing himself, first Wendy and then you!"

Piran came over to them and began pushing Peter's chair back up the path in silence. Anna wished urgently that someone would say something, anything, to take her mind off

Wendy. Jealousy is an ignoble emotion and she had nothing to be jealous about anyway. Did she *want* Piran to kiss her again?

Kynance Cove disappeared in the sea mist. Anna watched it blowing over the white sand and covering the little bit of the islands that she could see from the top. The mist came slowly up the cliffs to where they were standing and the world became suddenly cold and damp.

"Is it often misty here?" she asked Peter, more for something to say than because she thought he knew.

His dark eyes took in her quick shiver. "I believe you must have perjured your soul," he said solemnly. "That's what they say around here, that if you swear away a man's life, you'll never see or feel the sunshine ever again. The world will be perpetually grey –"

Piran smiled. "I knew a perjuror once. Grey of face and grey of nature!"

"What else can you expect?" Peter went on happily. "You'd better confess to your evil deeds!"

Anna giggled suddenly. "And I suppose you two are bathed in sunshine now!" she accused them.

Peter laughed. "We're perjured souls too. Aren't we, Piran?"

But the amusement had gone out of his father's face. He shoved the chair forward more quickly. "I wouldn't know," he said quietly. "I've often wondered about it."

The black, shut-down look came back to both Trethowyns. It was frankly a relief when they got back to the car and busied themselves with getting Peter and his chair into the front. It gave Anna a chance to take a last look at the serpentine shops, now filled with some tourists who had come to the Lizard on one of the coaches. There was a small model of St. Piran's cross, one of the ancient Celtic crosses of Cornwall, with a round top on a solid-looking standing stone. Anna looked at it longingly, admiring the colours in the serpentine from which it had been made. It was standing on some paper napkins patterned with various words from the Cornish language, with a label hanging on to it, saying what it was.

It took only a minute or two to go inside the shop and hand over the few coins that made the small celtic cross hers. She hid it in her handbag so that neither of the Trethowyns would see what she had bought. She thought she would keep it always, for to her it was a monument to Piran the man she knew, rather than Piran the saint she didn't know, other than what Peter had told her of his coming to Cornwall from Ireland, floating on a millstone, and that he had been a tinner as well as a powerful preacher. To Anna, Piran was a symbol of Cornwall to her, not as a patron saint or a legend or myth, but a man who was as unattainable to her as her mother's country had been all her life.

"Did you buy anything?" Peter asked with casual interest as she got into the car.

It was not natural to Anna not to speak the truth. "I looked at some of the things they had," she compromised.

Piran looked at her closely. "You have freckles on your nose," he told her.

She was put out that he had noticed. She fumbled in her handbag for her powder compact and obliterated them with a dusting of powder as quickly as she could.

"I like freckles," Peter remarked.

"Well, I don't!" Anna snapped.

"Naturally not!" Piran drawled.

"I don't see what's natural about it," she objected, and was crosser still when he laughed.

"One only sees freckles on the face of the girl next door," he teased her.

"I *am* the girl next door!" she reminded him haughtily.

"With good, wholesome freckles on your nose," he drawled. "And you're a liar to boot. I can see the package in your bag!"

She shut it with a bang, more harassed than she cared to admit. "It's none of your *business*!"

"None at all," he agreed smoothly. "Move over and I'll drive home."

"We want to go to Loe Bar," Peter put in.

"In this mist?" his father jeered. "Don't be ridiculous! We're going home."

Anna had to admit that he drove better than she did. He knew every road to a nicety and he put himself out to entertain her on the way by telling her all about the places they were passing, though she knew quite well that she would never remember one from the other.

"It's only a Celtic cross," she said.

"We call them Cornish crosses in Cornwall," he told her.

"I saw it in the window," she went on bravely.

"And you wanted it?"

She nodded. "I thought it would remind me of my first visit to the Lizard," she explained.

They came to a halt just outside Marazion, waiting for the heavy traffic to filter through the narrow streets. Piran put his hand in her handbag and drew out the little package. Slowly he unwrapped it and stood it on the palm of his hand.

"St. Piran's Cross," he said thoughtfully.

"Oh, is it?" She swallowed. "I – I hadn't noticed."

"No?" His eyes met hers and he laughed. "Oh, Anna! I wasn't very kind, was I? But you're to blame too! I'd like to believe in your niceness and your freckles –"

"But you can't?" she said.

"No, I can't," he agreed. He took off the brake and eased the

66

car forward a few feet further down the street. Anna sat beside him in silence, she wrapped up the small serpentine cross and put it back in her handbag. She was suddenly very tired and she longed for a hot cup of tea, on her own, somewhere far away from the Trethowyns. He had hurt her more badly than he knew.

CHAPTER FIVE

Of course there was nowhere she could go which was far away from the Trethowyns. As the days passed, Anna became more and more aware of this. It seemed to her that they came and went as they pleased, walking in and out of her cottage as though it was the most natural thing in the world. There was no escape from them. She tried burying herself in her work, but even then she would become aware of Peter's dark eyes staring at her, or, from her point of view worse still, Piran, faintly contemptuous of the articles she was turning out, would question her about her Cornish connections and the places she had visited and what she had seen.

Even so, she had not forgotten her idea of turning out little serpentine bottles, big enough for a single measure of mead in each, to see if it were possible to turn them out in anything like the numbers that Piran would need if he were to use them. She was busy drilling the soft, soapy marble when Peter knocked on her door and wheeled himself into her room.

"I've been to the doctor," he announced.

Anna's drill slipped and she swore softly under her breath. "Oh?" she said.

Peter picked up one of the little bottles that she had finished and examined it closely. She had drilled out the centre and polished the inside, leaving the outside rough round the middle, but polished at the bottom and round the mouth. A cork acted as a stopper until she could find something better.

"Have you shown these to Piran?" the boy asked her.

She shook her head. "No," she admitted, and blushed.

He put it back on the table, eyeing it sulkily. "Oh well, it's your affair. But I think you ought to mention it to Wendy. She'll be after your blood as it is."

Anna didn't believe him. She thought the Trethowyns thrived on trouble and would go a long way to meet it.

"I like Wendy," she stated firmly.

Peter laughed at her. "You would!" he jeered. "I never met such a simple-minded maid!"

Anna tried to look severe. "Peter! I'll not have you speaking to me like that!" she told him fiercely. "If you come here, you must be civil. And I don't appreciate your talking unkindly about other people either!"

The boy looked astonished. "I'm sorry," he muttered.

"Tell me what the doctor had to say," Anna encouraged him. It was not his fault that he had such a cynical view of life, she supposed.

"I have to do some exercises," he grunted.

"Well," she said brightly, "you expected that!"

"They hurt. They hurt intolerably."

"Did you ask him if they should?" she enquired. "Perhaps you're going about them the wrong way?"

Peter grimaced. "I should have been doing them all along," he confessed. "But somehow it never seemed worth it."

Anna's shocked eyes met his. "Why ever not?"

He shrugged. "You don't know how it is –"

"I know how the accident happened, if that's what you mean," she told him shyly. She turned on the electric drill to drown her words, because it suddenly seemed quite intolerable that she should know about Peter's mother and how she had died.

"Do you? I suppose Ellen told you? She didn't like my mother."

Anna turned the drill off again. "As a matter of fact your

uncle told me. Ellen only confirmed the fact that you were there because your mother couldn't bear your crying because she was going away. She said your mother had a very kind heart."

Peter coloured finely. "She was right!"

"Up to a point," Anna said carefully. "She didn't mind hurting Piran pretty badly, did she?"

"I don't think he was hurt!" Peter disclaimed. "He was glad to see us go. Glad to see us both go!"

"Are you sure?" Anna asked. She set the bottle she was working on down on the bench in front of her and studied it intently.

"Uncle Mike says —"

"What did your father say?" Anna cut him off.

"He was quite nice about things. He came up to London to get me, but I was in hospital and couldn't come straight back to Cornwall. I was only ten years old and it was pretty terrible in that hospital, I can tell you. I don't know what I would have done if Mike hadn't come to see me every day. It was almost as good as having my mother there, you see. They're so alike – they even look alike – looked alike!"

"Didn't your father stay in London too?"

Peter shook his head. "He was just starting up the business here. He said he couldn't afford to stay. He kept saying that he couldn't leave things here and that I would understand." His voice hardened with bitterness. "I understood all right. He hates London at the best of times and he certainly wasn't staying there just to entertain me. Besides, Mr. Morris decided against going in to the mead business with him and he had to talk Wendy into taking her father's place. I didn't care!"

"You had Mike!" Anna put in.

"Yes. He wanted me to go and live with him, but Piran

70

wouldn't allow that, so I had to come back here."

"But you didn't want to?"

"Not much. Piran hates my being crippled even more than I do. He blames my mother for it, but it wasn't her fault. *She* wasn't driving!"

"Did you tell him that?" Anna asked casually.

"Nobody ever asked me," he said. "They knew that she was going away with Jean-Baptiste and so they blamed her for everything! And she was dead and couldn't answer back!"

"It strikes me as a pretty rotten reason for staying a cripple," Anna said frankly. "I wouldn't want to stay in that wheelchair one second longer than I had to!"

Peter looked so angry that she was afraid she had gone too far. "You have no right –" he stormed at her.

"No right at all!" she agreed cheerfully.

"It wasn't because of *that* that I didn't do the exercises!"

Anna turned away from him and started to drill the next small bottle with immense care. It was a fiddlesome job that required intense concentration, if the drill wasn't to slip or go straight through the bottom.

"Truly it wasn't!" Peter insisted. "I don't care what Piran thinks about *anything*, so why should I want to be a cripple just to spite him?"

"It gives you a hold over him," Anna said.

Peter blenched. "I'm going to do the exercises now, aren't I?"

"Good," said Anna. "Do you want any help with them?"

His fists clenched until his knuckles were quite white. But it would be fatal to offer him any sympathy now, she decided.

"Why should you help me?" he demanded. "You don't even like me!"

Anna looked him straight in the face. "Do I have to like you?" she asked.

It was he who looked away. "You think I'm a pretty nasty person. I can tell. So why bother with me at all?"

Anna smiled at him. "I can't think!" she said. "Perhaps I don't think you are really as nasty as all that. Besides, you're my landlord. I can hardly ignore you when you come for the rent, can I?"

A reluctant smile touched his lips. "Do you laugh at everybody?" he asked her.

"No," she admitted. She hadn't laughed at all when Piran had kissed her. "But my mother used to. You would have liked her. It's a pity she didn't know about you when you were in hospital —"

"What happened to her?" he asked, his interest caught. It hadn't occurred to him that Anna had a family and a life of her own quite apart from what he knew of her in Cornwall.

"She's dead too," Anna said softly. "She knew she was dying for a long time. I tried to make it as nice for her as I could, but we didn't have very much money and I was working all the time. She spent a great deal of time on her own. She would have liked to have had someone to talk to."

Peter was genuinely upset at the thought of anyone being on their own like that. "I bet she'd have made me do my exercises too!" he said, trying to be funny.

Anna laughed. "Could be! What do you have to do?"

He explained each exercise at length and what it was supposed to do for him. Anna was silent. She had known that he must have been badly hurt, but it was only now that she realised how badly mangled his legs had been. They had operated, of course, and had done much to strengthen his thigh muscles and to reform those which had been completely severed, but their efforts had taken a long time to heal and the boy had been growing all the time. The exercises were needed now to build up the muscles he had left, so that one

72

day they would take the weight of his body and allow him to walk again.

"I have to have physiotherapy too," he ended. "The doctor is arranging it at the local hospital."

"Good for you!" she congratulated him, pleased.

"The thing is," he added, "I wondered if you'd drive me to the hospital when I have to go? Would you mind?"

Anna smiled at him. "I'd like to," she said.

The boy heaved a great sigh of relief. "That's all right then," he said.

Anna was in a complacent mood. She had completed the first of her major assignments for London and she was in the comfortable position of knowing that the quality of the goods she had sent was good. Some of the pieces were the best she had ever done, based on some designs she had found in the museum at Penzance of some prehistoric jewellery that had been discovered in the area. Made mostly of gold, they were exotic and barbaric. With only a few modifications they had become modern jewellery at its very best.

It was hot, though, waiting for Peter outside the hospital. In the cottage she had so arranged things that she could always get a through draught of some sort, but it was different in the streets of Penzance. There nothing stirred and the sun blazed down without hindrance on to the crowds that struggled from shop to shop. Anna had already done her shopping. She had climbed the steps on to the raised pavement and had hurried from shop to shop to get finished as quickly as she could. Now she had nothing more to do than to wait for Peter to come out of the hospital.

She filled in her time by dawdling in a sketching block. She had long ago discovered that this was the best way of designing the jewellery she made. Details she had half forgotten that

73

she had ever seen arrived suddenly on the paper, completing some half thought out design. Or, if what she was drawing didn't fit together, it was easy enough to scratch it out and start again.

She was concentrating so hard on what she was doing that she didn't notice another car draw in beside her until Piran got out of it and came striding over to where she was sitting.

"Where's Peter?" he demanded.

Anna's eyes widened. "D-didn't he tell you?"

"No."

She sighed. "He's in the physiotherapy department. He'll be out in a minute."

"And you're acting as his chauffeur?"

"It suits both of us," she answered stiffly. Surely he must be pleased that his son was at last doing his exercises properly.

"Maybe," he retorted. "But *I'll* drive him home. You can take the other car. Here's the key."

Anna got out on to legs that felt strangely wobbly and insecure.

"You'll be nice to him, won't you?" she pleaded with him.

Piran didn't answer. In silence, he helped her transfer her packages to the other car. She noticed his surprise at the weight of a lump of lead she had purchased and his disapproval of the casual way she had twisted an ingot of gold into a sheet of newspaper. She needed the gold to fashion the settings she used for some of the more valuable stones. It was only nine-carat gold, not really very valuable when compared to the purer golds of twenty and even twenty-two carats that was used for diamonds, rubies, emeralds, sapphires, the aristocrats of the precious stones.

"He thinks you find it embarrassing having a cripple for a son," she added diffidently. "Did you know that?"

"It was reasonably obvious!" he retorted.

She clenched her teeth. She would have liked to have hit him. She might have done so had it not been for the hurt look at the back of his eyes. When all was said and done, she thought, Peter was his son and he should have been told. But not by her! It was not her business to tell him about Peter. Surely he must realise that?

She got into the smaller car and drove off without a backward glance. The gears were on the floor and not on the steering column as they were in the other car, and she had some difficulty with them as she changed down to tackle the hill out of Penzance.

She was surprised to find a fresh breeze blowing when she got out of the car and carried her purchases across the Trethowyn garden to her own cottage. The door of the cabin was standing open and so she was able to walk straight inside and deposit the packages on the nearest table. It was only by degrees that she realised that she was not alone. Sitting on the settle in the hearth was Michael Vaynor. He had a glass in his hand and, without bothering to get to his feet, he silently toasted her.

"Our busy little neighbour returns!" he greeted her.

She went on sorting out her packages. "How did you get in?" she asked him.

"The door was unlocked." He grinned at her. "Am I unwelcome?" He knew that he was and he enjoyed taunting her with the knowledge. "Shall I go?" he offered.

She shook her head. "Not if you don't want to," she replied coolly. "What are you drinking?"

"I found it in your kitchen. I think it's cider. I've made quite a hole in it, I'm afraid. But then I've been waiting for you for quite a long time."

Anna went into the kitchen and poured herself out a glass

75

of the cider, draining the bottle. It had been full when she had gone out. Michael Vaynor must have been in the cabin for some time. She went back to the sitting-room and sat down on the wooden chair that stood opposite him in the hearth.

"Well?" she said.

He smiled slowly. "You make a refreshing change for these parts," he said whimsically. "I'm intrigued to know how you're getting on with the worthy Piran. I would have thought that a beautiful girl would have been an object of intense suspicion as far as he was concerned, yet here you are, still welcome in the Trethowyn abode!"

"I don't see very much of Piran," she said.

"No, of course not," he agreed readily. The charming liveliness drained from his face. "But you do of Peter?" he snapped at her.

"Why not?" she retorted.

"Because I don't wish it," he said. "I don't like it at all. I prefer Peter's affection to be mine, you understand. He had very little in common with Piran and that suits me very well. There's no need for you to come along and poke your nose into things that are none of your business. I thought I'd drop in and warn you."

"I see," said Anna gently.

"I don't suppose you do, my pet," he went on. "Shall we just say that I very much dislike having my toes trodden on? Keep away from Peter of your own accord and we'll get along just fine, otherwise I shall have to step in and have you sent back to London."

Anna took a sip of cider. "I don't think you could do that," she said.

"Don't you?" How very handsome he was, she thought, with his fair, lightly tanned skin stretched tight over his cheekbones. Perhaps his mouth was rather over-full for a man, but as he

76

smiled so often it was not very noticeable.

"No, I don't," she said.

"I'll find a way," he assured her. "I imagine there's nothing official about your tenancy here, for instance? It would be easy enough to have you turned out, and then where would you go?"

Anna took a deep breath. She had the advantage of knowing that she had a legal contract to rent the cabin for a full year. Oddly, she remembered, it had been Piran who had insisted on that.

"What do you imagine I can do to Peter?" she enquired calmly.

He frowned. "I don't know. But the boy isn't the same as he was. It will be best for everyone when he comes and lives with me in London. Ellen tells me he's been getting ideas recently that he might walk again –"

"Don't you think he will?" she asked him sharply.

"Of course not!" He dismissed the idea a little too easily. "I should have thought it was obvious. The boy needs a stable background with someone to see about his real interests, not encourage him in idle dreams!"

Anna suppressed a laugh. "I thought Piran was his father," she said with intentional sarcasm.

"He had a Vaynor for his mother! And the money he inherited from her is Vaynor money! Why should Piran get his hands on it?"

"Why should you?" Anna riposted.

"It's *my* money!" he insisted.

She laughed out loud at that. She couldn't believe that Peter had inherited much money anyway. If he had, why should Piran have had such a struggle to get his Meadhouse going? Why, too, should the house be in such a run-down condition?

"Look! I'm being nice to you!" Michael shouted at her.

"I've given you the benefit of the doubt ever since you got here –"

"The benefit of what doubt?" she interrupted him, still smiling.

"I thought you came here by chance," he answered. "An innocent who'd walked into the Trethowyn mess with your eyes tight shut. I even thought you didn't like Piran too much, not at first. But it wasn't true, was it? You couldn't keep your meddling fingers out of it, could you?"

Her laughter died away. "Why should it matter to you?" she asked him.

"I'm explaining it to you," he went on. "I'm not allowing Piran to get his hands on the Vaynor money. The money is mine, do you understand that? It so happens that the money is attached to the boy, therefore the boy is going to be mine too! Is that clear enough for you?"

She blinked. "No," she retorted. "I don't understand at all!"

"You don't want to," he accused her. "The money belonged to my sister. She was so determined that Piran wasn't going to get it that she ran away, taking the boy with her, because she'd made him her heir. *That* was why she ran away!"

"And the Frenchman?"

"The Frenchman was incidental."

Anna gazed at him in complete disbelief. "How do you know?" she chided him.

"I knew my sister. Neurotic as all the Vaynor women always are, but faithful in her own fashion. She never would have gone if she had thought that Piran really wanted her, but it was pretty clear that he didn't! So she wasn't going to let him get his hands on the money as well. The boy and the money were *hers*, not his!"

Anna noticed that her hand shook badly as she lifted her

78

tumbler of cider to her lips. She was doubly annoyed by the fact: annoyed that she was afraid of this man; and annoyed that it should show so clearly, so that he could hardly be unaware of the fact.

"I don't think that any of this is my business," she said in a strained voice.

"It isn't," he agreed heartily. "Only you couldn't leave well alone, could you? You had to interfere –"

"In what way?" she asked indignantly.

"The boy! You had to see that he did his exercises, didn't you? You even took it on yourself to build up some sort of relationship between him and his father!"

"And what if I did?"

Michael shook his finger at her, thus irritating her beyond measure. "It shows you have the instincts of a busybody!"

"You mean," she retorted, "that it doesn't happen to suit you!"

"Same thing, sweetie, same thing!"

"Not to me, Mr. Vaynor. I'm sorry to ask you to go, but I really prefer not to listen to you –"

"You haven't any choice," he answered her, no longer charming, and yet he still looked handsome in that golden, antiseptic way that she disliked so much.

"Mr. Vaynor, please go," she said with dignity. Her eyes met his and held them.

"Now then, my pretty one, there's no need to blow your top. I'm sure we can come to a very satisfactory agreement – with a little bit of good will." He smiled at her. "You're not above a little bit of fun, are you?"

Anna didn't deign to answer him. She put her drink down on the floor and rose to her feet. Too late did she see that that was a mistake, for he stood up too, blocking off her exit from the hearth.

79

"Mr. Vaynor," she said gently, "please get out of my way."

"It's *you* who's in my way," he answered silkily.

"Rubbish!" she said crossly. "How could I be?"

He laughed and the sound of it grated on her ears. "I don't intend that you shall be for long," he told her. "I hadn't realised at our first meeting what a pretty little thing you are. Not quite the sophisticated siren of my choice perhaps, but pretty enough! Certainly you're the loveliest thing around here –"

"There's Wendy," she reminded him mildly. If there was one thing she loathed, it was the kind of man who held you against your will.

"The redoubtable Wendy is *not* in my way," he said. "In fact I think she wants very much the same thing as I do. Piran becomes immediately more desirable the less she has to remember that he was once married to my sister. Haven't you noticed what an aversion she has to sharing her possessions?"

Anna tossed up in her mind whether it was worth trying to push past him. She decided against it, for she didn't want to touch him if she could help it.

"Mr. Vaynor, I –"

"Michael," he prompted her. "Mike if you like."

"Mr. Vaynor," she repeated sternly. "Peter will be back from the hospital in a minute. I presume it was him that you really came to see?"

"You're too modest!" he mocked her.

"Really?" she sighed.

"Shall I prove it to you?" she asked. "I can, quite easily, you know."

"I think not," she answered.

"Little prude!" he muttered. He stepped forward and grasped her awkwardly, pulling her into his arms. "Anyone would think you didn't like being kissed!" he growled.

"I don't," she said positively.

"You can pretend you're cold with any other man, sweetie, but not with me!" he said bitterly. "I'll show you!"

There was no escaping him and to struggle would only have encouraged him. Anna knew a moment's complete disgust as he pressed his mouth down on hers and she shivered compulsively, hating his touch and his bruising fingers on her arms. When he let her go, she put a hand up to her mouth and gave him a look of such complete dislike that for a moment he looked puzzled.

"Please go away, Mr. Vaynor!" she repeated.

He forced a laugh. "You're very sure of yourself! But this is a battle I intend to win, my dear!"

Anna's quick ears picked up the sound of approaching footsteps coming through the gap in the fuchsia hedge and she could have cried with relief. Perhaps it would be Ellen bringing her some of the mint and other herbs she had promised her. But it was not Ellen, for the footsteps were too heavy to be hers. They paused for a instant, but not before Michael Vaynor had heard them too.

"How very convenient," he said in Anna's ear. His arms went round her once again and he kissed her once more just as Piran came in through the door.

Anna struggled free, her face scarlet. "*Now* will you go?" she asked desperately.

He smiled slowly, his triumph naked in his eyes. "Seeing that you've been so nice to me –" He paused significantly. "Why, Piran, how you do creep about!" He walked slowly to the door, put his hat on at a jaunty angle on his head, and walked away.

"Why couldn't you have come earlier?" Anna stormed at Piran, afraid she would break down and cry.

"And interrupt your pleasure?" Piran drawled. "That isn't

quite my line. I made that mistake last time, if you remember."

"Then why come at all?" Anna asked him.

His mouth twisted into the facsimile of a smile. "I came to thank you," he said. "I'm sorry my timing is so bad."

"But you can't think that I liked his kissing me?" she almost pleaded with him.

He raised his eyebrows thoughtfully. "Can't I?"

"But he's horrible!"

Piran shook his head at her slowly. "And was I horrible too?" he asked.

There was nothing she could say to that. She sat down on the wooden settle and stared at him in silence for a long moment. "No," she said, "you weren't horrible. I never said you were!"

He put his tongue in his cheek, his eyes black with contempt. "That's what I thought," he said.

CHAPTER SIX

ANNA swore to herself that she would have nothing more to do with any of the Trethowyns after that. For two whole days she solemnly locked the door of the cabin whether she was in or out. Once or twice she heard Peter's chair outside, but she pretended that she hadn't and, after a while, he went away. She couldn't help wondering if he was hurt and worrying about whether he was going to physiotherapy and even if he was doing his exercises properly. It was one thing to swear off his father and his uncle; it was another to dismiss Peter from her affections in the same casual way.

It was Piran, though, who put an end to her solitude. It was inevitable that sooner or later she would forget to lock her door and, when she did, she came home to find him sitting on the settle in the hearth, the little stone bottles she had made arrayed around his feet.

"When did you do these?" he asked, just as if their last conversation had never taken place.

"Whenever I had nothing else to do," she answered. She made an effort to sound as cool and indifferent as possible, but it was difficult to judge what success she had had, for all his attention was concentrated on those wretched bottles.

"What capacity have they?" he barked at her.

She clenched her hands together. "They'll each hold a single measure of mead," she said.

He looked up and grinned at her. "That's what I thought," he agreed.

She was embarrassed. "It was only an experiment to see if it was possible to make them out of serpentine," she muttered.

"They're not for you!"

He raised his black brows a fraction. "No?"

"No," she said flatly.

"But they're ideal! And very pretty! What *do* you intend to do with them?"

Anna turned her back on him. "I don't see that that's any of your business!" she snapped.

He laughed. He seemed different, she thought. But perhaps it was only the lack of bitterness in his speech. The Trethowyns were often bitter.

"Why don't you show them to Wendy?" he suggested.

"I might," she admitted. "I don't want to tread on her toes."

He gave her a quick look. "You won't do that. Besides," he added, "I'll smooth her ruffled feathers down again. Wendy never holds a grudge for long – not where the business is concerned. Look, why don't I take one of these bottles with me to show it to her?"

"If you like," she said awkwardly. The coldness that had gripped her insides like a vice for the last few days cracked a little. "But perhaps you'd better not tell her where you got it from."

"All right, I won't," he agreed promptly. He slipped one of the little bottles into the pocket of his jacket and stood up. "By the way, I really came to ask you if you'd like to come out with Peter and me in the boat?"

"H-have you got a boat?" she stalled. It was something, she supposed, that Peter and his father did anything willingly together.

Piran smiled at her. "Didn't you know?"

She shook her head. "What sort of boat?"

"It isn't very grand. Peter and I sail her quite a bit, and she has an engine as well. Peter does most of the steering now because he can sit at the back and get on with it without too much difficulty –"

"And Mr. Vaynor?" she interrupted him.

It was impossible to tell what he was thinking, for his dark eyes were completely enigmatic as he looked at her. "Mike doesn't care for little boats. They make him sick," he told her, not without satisfaction.

Her mouth twitched. She tried to stop herself from laughing, but failed. To her surprise, he began to laugh too.

"I'd love to come!" she said.

He was still smiling. "I believe you think I'm being clever, finding something that the boy prefers doing with me," he drawled, amused. "Would you prefer it if Mike came along?"

"No!"

The explosive negative intrigued him, but Anna showed no signs of elaborating on it and something in the expression on her face forbade him to press the matter further.

"Have you ever done any shark fishing?" he asked.

She shook her head silently. She was afraid of sharks. It wasn't that she had ever seen one, except one stuffed in a museum, but the stories she had heard about them had not done anything to encourage her to like them.

"Is that what you use the boat for?"

"Why, yes," he said. "It's tremendous fun! Peter and I will expect you this afternoon. All right?"

She nodded slowly, unwilling that he should see that she was afraid. "All right," she said.

When he was gone the cottage seemed bare and empty. Anna was accustomed to a lonely life and she never remembered before minding how much time she spent alone, and yet, for the first few minutes after she had seen him into his own garden through the fuchsia hedge, she felt truly bereft. There was a full hour before she need change her clothes and for quite half that time she mooned about the cabin, fingering this and that

piece of jewellery, trying to consider the necklace she was trying to make, but coming back again and again to the little
serpentine bottles she had made for Piran.

It was the longest hour of her life. She made a point of laying out her jeans and shirt on her bed and making sure that
she had some strong, light shoes that wouldn't slip on the wet
decks. In the end she had to hurry into her clothes in order
to be ready in time when Peter came across the lawn to fetch
her.

"We're taking Wendy too," he whispered to her in an under-
tone. "She and Piran have quarrelled and he wants to make it
up with her."

"Quarrelled?" Anna repeated vaguely, and then as the
words sank in, "What on earth have they quarrelled about?"

"How should I know?" Peter protested.

Wendy and Piran were already waiting in the car; Piran in
the driving seat and Wendy, her face devoid of all expression,
in the seat behind him. Piran got out when he saw them coming and waved to Anna to get in beside Wendy while he swung
Peter and his chair up into the space beside him.

Wendy was dressed in a skirt, with a light, frilly blouse only
barely visible under her cardigan that was buttoned up to the
neck despite the hot weather. As Anna got in, she pulled her
skirt away, pushing it carefully under her leg in case Anna
should touch her.

"I do think you might have brought your idea of serpentine
bottles to me!" she said immediately.

"I would have done in time," Anna answered calmly.

"But the fact of the matter is that you didn't!" Wendy complained. "I'm in charge of that side of things, you know, not
Piran."

"Yes, I did know," Anna said gently. "Truly, I would have
brought them to you first, but Piran found them in my sitting-

room and, naturally, he was interested. What did you think of them?"

Only slightly mollified, Wendy sniffed. "I don't think they're practical," she objected at once. "And *far* too expensive!"

Anna smiled. "Could be," she said indifferently.

"Aren't you interested?" Wendy demanded.

"Not very," Anna admitted. "I wanted to see if it was possible to make little bottles out of serpentine. I don't much care whether they are filled with a nip of mead, or scent, or anything else."

"But it was seeing the Meadhouse hat gave you the idea!" Wendy accused her.

"Mmm," Anna agreed. "Some of your bottles are putting across the Cornish side, but I don't like them much, do you?"

"Of course I do! We wouldn't sell them otherwise. Not everyone has your odd idea that stone is nicer than other things that can be really pretty!"

Anna swallowed. She didn't know what to say if Wendy really did prefer little plastic animals to the lovely, subtle colours of the soapy marble of the Lizard. "Perhaps there's room for both?" she suggested amiably.

Wendy glared at her. "If you can make them economic," she said in triumph. "Piran's estimate was far too high. No one would pay a price like that!"

Peter turned his head to hear what the two girls were talking about while his father went round the front of the car and got in behind the steering wheel. "A price like what?" he asked.

Wendy looked crosser than ever. "It's none of *your* business!" she told the boy. "You'd only take Miss St. James' side! We all know that!"

Peter made a face at Anna before turning back to his father.

"Do you know what it's all about?" he asked him.

"I can guess," Piran grunted.

"Well, it matters!" Wendy complained.

Piran turned right round and looked at her. "You're right, as ever, my love! We need someone to look out for our interests all the time. I was lucky to find you to do it for me –"

"I knew you'd come round!" she said with satisfaction. "It isn't only in your work you need someone to guard your interests –"

Piran smiled. "Are you volunteering?" he drawled.

Wendy coloured faintly. "You know I'd do it anyway," she said.

Piran reached for the gear lever and started up the engine. The car slipped forward up the slope of the drive. "Yes, I know," he said.

The boat was in the harbour at Penzance. Piran let them all out of the car beside the Promenade and drove off to park the car. Anna pushed Peter's wheelchair along the pink, newly made-up area. If she looked over her shoulder, she could see the road that led out of Newlyn, beside a quarry to Mousehole. Away out to sea the salvage boat stood at its station, ever on the alert for ships in trouble.

There was a gaggle of fishing boats coming and going at the entrance to the harbour, their PZ markings clearly visible from the quay. Peter pointed out their own boat with excitement. To Anna, it looked old and badly in need of a coat of paint. Most of the decks were littered with pieces of rope and heavy canvas sails of a dull rust colour. A few dead fish had been left in a bucket in the cockpit and, looking through a porthole, she could see the table inside the cabin was covered with half-cleaned sea-urchins.

"Piran was out in her yesterday," Peter said by way of explanation.

"Oh," said Anna.

She and Wendy managed to get on board, but there was no way that she could see of getting Peter anywhere near the boat until Piran came along.

"Perhaps we could clean up a little bit," she said to Wendy.

The other girl shrugged her shoulders. "I do so hate getting my clothes dirty," she complained. "Will you just look at the state of that cabin?" She shuddered. "There's nowhere to sit at all!"

The bucket of dead fish gave out a smell that was enough to put anyone off, Anna thought. She wondered what would happen if she were to tip the decomposing contents over the side, but when she lifted up the bucket Peter began to shout something at her.

"It smells!" she shouted back.

"It's meant to smell!" he retorted. "That's the 'rubby-dubby'!"

A small diversion was caused by Piran's arrival. Together with a friendly fisherman, he lowered Peter into the cockpit of the boat and jumped aboard himself. He eased Peter into his seat in front of the wheel. The seat was a good one for the purpose, for it revolved round easily and yet was firm and bolted to the deck so that nothing could overturn it.

"If you don't get rid of that fish, I shall throw up!" Wendy announced suddenly.

Piran grinned at her. "We'll need it for bait," he said.

"Then put it somewhere else!" she insisted.

Anna's own stomach felt decidedly queasy, but she knew that once they got going the breeze would clear the stench away from the boat, so she said nothing. To be thought poor-spirited was a worse fate, she thought, than to be stunned by a particularly disagreeable smell.

Peter laughed. "Neither of them appreciate the rubby-dubby!" he told his father. "Cast off quickly before they change their minds and go home!"

The boy started up the engine and watched smiling while Piran cast off, showing Anna how to curl the ropes neatly out of their way. Peter pushed the gear stick forward, revving up the engine until they turned completely round in their own length and headed out to sea. Anna found herself a seat and sat down quickly until she got used to the motion of the boat and found out what was wanted of her. Piran was busy with the sails, talking and laughing with Peter just like any other father and son. If they were left alone, she thought, not without indignation, they could well become very good friends. Only Wendy wasn't sure what to do or where to do it. She tried, rather ineffectually, to help Piran with the sails, hanging on to his shoulder to keep his balance. Anna was amused to notice the impatient expression on his face. Serve him right! she thought.

When they got away from the harbour the sea suddenly caught them. Anna could feel the deep water dragging at the bottom of the boat beneath her feet and she felt suddenly completely alive. Peter tilted his face to meet the wind and shouted something to his father.

"If you like," Piran replied.

Peter pushed the gear lever into the neutral position and the boat shifted with the waves like a cork on a pond.

"Come and help!" Piran commanded the two girls.

Anna hauled on the ropes with a will, her spirits lifting with the sails. She had never been on a sailing boat of any size before and so she had never experienced the exciting moment when the wind fills the sails and sends the craft skimming across the water. The silence after the noise of the engine, with only the slapping of the waves against the bow and the faint trickle of the water falling away behind the stern. It was the most wonderful sensation she had even known.

"What is the rubby-dubby for?" she asked Piran.

He grinned with amusement. "We drop it overboard to attract the sharks to the boat. The first thing we have to do is to catch some mackerel for bait, though. Peter is taking us out to our favourite ground now."

Anna sighed with sheer pleasure. "I could go on sailing for ever!" she exclaimed.

He cast a quick eye over her. "So I see!" he observed. "I wish I could say the same for Wendy."

Anna's conscience smote her, for she hadn't given the other girl a single thought since they had raised the sails. She looked thoroughly miserable now. Her skirt blew in the wind, making her self-conscious, and she looked as if she were about to be sick at any moment.

"Haven't you taken her out before?" Anna asked Piran disapprovingly.

He shook his head. "On a boat? Never!"

"I'll make her a hot drink," Anna offered. "She'll feel better with something warm inside her."

Piran nodded without much interest. "You'll find all the things in the cabin," he told her.

Anna stood up, dodged the boom as it went over her head, and bent almost double to get through the door into the small cabin. She wrinkled up her nose in disgust at the sea-urchins which littered the table. Only one or two had been properly cleaned of its spines, leaving the pretty pink and mauve shell which makes such a fine ornament. Anna examined one which still had its spines intact. It was easy to see why they are sometimes called sea-hedgehogs. It was rather less easy to see why they should have been thought to be mermaids' eggs, but perhaps that was only a romantic story to intrigue the credulous.

She managed to clear a space on the table and then turned

91

her attention to the small Calor gas stove. It lit easily tnough and she pumped up some water into the kettle and put it on the stove to boil. There was no coffee that she could find, but there was a tin of drinking chocolate and some dried milk. She blended the two together and poured the boiling water on top into the four mugs she had found in a cupboard. She picked up two of the mugs and leaned out into the cockpit to attract Wendy's attention.

"Shall I come in there to drink it?" Wendy asked pathetically.

Anna stood back to allow her to enter. "You look cold!" she exclaimed.

"I never would have come if I'd known what it was like!" Wendy cried. "I'm *frozen*!"

Anna felt her hands and was dismayed to discover that she was shivering. "You'd better borrow Piran's coat," she advised her. She put the tweed coat around the other girl's shoulders and settled her firmly on the single bunk out of the wind. "I shan't be a minute," she said, "I'll just take the others their chocolate."

"Aren't you cold at all?" Wendy complained.

Anna shook her head. "Boats make some people cold," she said. She didn't know it for a fact, but she thought that she had read something about it at one time.

"I thought it would please Piran if I came," Wendy went on. "But he's hardly noticed that I'm here —"

"He wouldn't have asked you if he hadn't wanted you," Anna consoled her. "You'll feel better in a minute."

"At the moment I wish I were dead!" Wendy said flatly.

Anna sighed. "Why on earth did you come?" she asked.

Wendy cast her a speaking glance. "Why do you suppose?" She reached out a hand for her mug of hot chocolate, her charm bracelet tinkling. She made a face as she looked at the dark brown liquid, screwing up her face to drink it. "Somehow, I hadn't thought of you as naïve!" she added dryly.

"Nor had I!" Anna agreed, her tone equally dry. "I suppose you're in love with him?"

Wendy nodded gloomily. "I have been all my life," she confirmed.

Anna's eyes smarted with sudden tears. "And he?" she asked.

"He'll come round. If only we could get Peter settled. He said as much the other day! Some nonsense about not presenting Peter with a stepmother that he didn't like. Well, we all know that Peter doesn't like me much and that he's longing to go off with his Uncle Mike, so what else could Piran have meant?"

"I don't know," Anna said. "I don't think he'll let Peter go."

"Then you don't know Piran!" Wendy said in triumph.

No, Anna admitted to herself, she did not. The Trethowyns intrigued and bewildered her, but she certainly did not understand them. She liked them a little; occasionally she thought she might love them a lot; but most of the time she was painfully aware of their unconscious ability to hurt her. It was not their fault, she excused them. It was her own fault for being so miserably vulnerable where they were concerned. She smiled with cautious amusement at herself. Neither she nor Wendy were going to get much happiness out of the situation, she thought. But, although that should have given the two girls something in common, it couldn't make them like each other one pennyworth more, which was a pity, for Wendy was the only girl that Anna had met who was about her own age in Cornwall. If either of them had been different people, they might have been friends, exchanging gossip over the teacups, and –

"I think I'm going to be sick!" Wendy cried out piteously.

Anna looked at her green face and her sympathy overcame her dislike for the other girl. "Perhaps you'll feel better when you have been sick," she said.

Wendy gave her a look of acute dislike. "Oh, get out!" she moaned. "If I'm going to die, I certainly don't want you around to watch me on my deathbed, thank you very much!"

Anna grinned. She didn't think Wendy could be feeling quite as bad as she looked, and anyway, she was only too glad to leave the cabin and go out into the fresh air. She stuck her head out first and looked about her. They were not very far from the land, sailing across Mount's Bay towards the Lizard. Just off the port bow stood the fabled St. Michael's Mount. The castle gleamed golden in the sun, towering above the private gardens and the dark green trees. From the sea, the whole island looked wilder and more aloof than it did from the busy beach of Marazion. From there, with the causeway and the harbour and the neat houses of the men and women who worked on the Mount, it was comparatively gentle and domestic. No storms whipped themselves up and smote that side of the island, but from the sea there was nothing to protect it from the Atlantic storms and the prevailing south-west winds.

"Where are we going?" she asked Peter.

The boy nodded towards the cabin. "How is she?" he asked.

Anna nearly smiled. "Sick," she said.

Peter tried to stop a laugh, failed, and gave up, his whole body shaking. "Poor Wendy!" he whooped.

"It's very unpleasant for her," Anna said in reproving tones.

Peter laughed all the harder. "Oh, boy!" he exclaimed. "Piran doesn't have much luck, does he?"

"Don't!" Anna protested.

The boy's laughter died away. "Why should you care?" he asked suspiciously.

"I don't!" Anna retorted sharply.

"No?" It was obvious Peter didn't believe her. "Cheer up," he advised her, "I much prefer you!" He blinked, frowning at the horizon. "Not that it counts for anything, of course," he added.

Anna smiled gently. "It counts with me," she said.

He was inordinately pleased though he shied away from any show of emotion. He brought the boat about with considerable skill, concentrating every thought on what he was doing.

"Why don't you go forward with Piran?" he suggested gruffly. "We'll be going in to Prussia Cove in a minute and he can show you the seals sunning themselves on the rocks."

"He might be busy –" she began hesitantly.

But Peter brushed her objections aside. "Hi, Piran! Come and show this landlubber the sights!"

His father looked up and grinned. "Okay," he grunted, "if you think you can sail the boat all by yourself?"

"I can," Peter assured him.

Piran smiled lazily. "The confidence of youth!" he mocked. "Come on, Anna, leave him to it! The worst he can do is to run us on to the rocks."

Anna climbed the short ladder and ran across the canvas deck that acted as the roof of the cabin. Some instinct made her move as quietly as possible. It was because she didn't want Wendy to come out, she knew, but she was rather ashamed of wanting to exclude the other girl, who must be feeling pretty miserable anyway. Piran moved over to allow her to sit beside him on the narrow foredeck. His dark eyes smiled faintly at her.

"Satisfied?" he asked her.

She jumped. "What do you mean?" she countered.

"What I said. Are you satisfied that I do care what Peter thinks and does?"

Anna blushed. "I think we agreed that it isn't any of my business," she said stiffly.

"Didn't I apologise for that?" he said blandly.

"No."

"And women always claim their pound of flesh!" he accused her in a voice suddenly grown tired.

Anna sat up very straight. "It depends on the woman," she said carefully. "Don't you think?"

"Does it?" He was silent for an instant. "Perhaps I haven't been very lucky in the women I've known. Tell me about yourself, Anna. What do you demand of life?"

She didn't like the question. "I don't think I demand anything very much," she answered.

"Not even a man to keep you in comfort for the rest of your life?"

She shook her head. "Not that! You see, I like doing my work. Besides," she added with a touch of humour, "I'm quite well off now that I only have myself to support."

He looked at her, his interest caught. "I don't know much about you, do I?" he confessed apologetically.

"There isn't much to know," she said quickly. "I think I'd better see how Wendy is. I don't think she likes little boats any better than Mr. Vaynor does!"

Piran chuckled unfeelingly. "Ask her if she wants to be put ashore at Prussia Cove!" he called after her.

She would most certainly do nothing of the sort, she thought indignantly. Peter brought the boat about again and, in dodging the boom, she fell to her hands and knees. From her new vantage point she could see the boy clearly, the muscles of his back and shoulders rippling in the sun as he sailed the boat confidently and competently towards the Lizard. It was then that she realised that he was *using his legs*! He had wedged them against the side of the boat and as they dipped and rose, settling to their new course, he pushed hard with his legs the better to keep his balance. Anna lay on her stomach and watched him for a long time, a wild hope rising within her.

She was unaware of Piran as he dropped down beside her.

"What are you looking at?" he asked her.

"It's Peter," she breathed. "Did you know that he uses his legs when he brings the boat about?"

Piran shook his head. He was silent for such a long time that she grew restive and began to struggle to her feet again. Piran didn't move. He lay flat on his stomach, his face hidden in his arms, and, for one awful moment, she thought he was crying.

CHAPTER SEVEN ·

WENDY refused Piran's offer to put her ashore at Prussia Bay.

"It wouldn't worry you, of course, that I would have to wait hours for a bus! Just who do you think you are, Piran Trethowyn? I suppose the atmosphere of the place makes you think you can act like the smugglers of old?"

"I shouldn't dream of it," Piran answered lazily. "They were a ruthless bunch of men!"

"And you're not?" Wendy returned sweetly.

Piran grunted. "I think not," he said.

Peter looked impatiently from one to the other of them. "Why don't we get on with it?" he asked.

"Because Anna hasn't gone ashore and picked up the mackerel," Piran told him lazily. "We did elect her for the job, didn't we?"

"I didn't hear you!" Anna said flatly.

Piran grinned at her. "I'll help you, if you like?"

Anna looked eagerly about her. She had never before seen a genuine smuggler's cove like this one. It was not difficult to imagine Captain Henry Carter, the "King of Prussia", and his bride from Helford, slipping in and out of this slit in the cliffs. Nor was it difficult to see why the revenue men had found it so difficult to capture him. It was a very harrow harbour, with a steep path rising up the cliff at the top of which were a couple of ancient shacks, their thatched roofs collapsing into the old stone framework that had once supported them.

Piran pointed up at the cabins. "I arranged for some mackerel to be left up there for us," he said.

"It would have been simpler to catch our own," Peter retorted.

His father chuckled. "I'm not sure I don't agree with you!" he said.

He held the boat steady by the rocks so that the girls could jump ashore. There was no quay in the cove, only a slipway on which the boat could be beached, but the Trethowyn sloop was rather big for such a course. Anna jumped easily ashore and turned to help Wendy to follow her. The other girl scorned her help, however, landing nimbly on a nearby rock and leaping easily down onto the slipway.

"I'll race you to the top!" she called out to Piran.

"You're on!" he said. "Coming, Anna?"

Something in Wendy's eyes made Anna shake her head. "I'll wait here," she said. "Racing up precipices is not my scene."

He laughed. "I'm not sure it's mine either," he admitted. "But the scenery is rather splendid from the top."

Wendy, who had recovered her spirits now that the boat was no longer pitching and tossing on the water, said lightly, "I'm complimented, Piran!"

Anna turned away from the sight of them, teasing one another, and running up the steep path, sometimes one ahead and sometimes the other. She fastened the painter to a metal loop in one of the rocks and climbed wearily back on board.

"Why didn't you go with them?" Peter asked her. "I would have been all right."

She shrugged her shoulders. "I thought they might want to be alone," she said.

Peter raised his eyebrows significantly. "The trouble with you, Anna, is that you're too nice!"

"That's what you think!" Anna retorted.

Peter smiled. "Wendy is a determined sort of person," he said. "Actually I don't think you stand a chance!"

"Perhaps I don't want to!" Anna claimed fiercely.

Peter laughed at her openly. "No?" he said.

"Do you like Wendy?" she asked him curiously. If she was to be his stepmother it would help if there was some affection between them, Anna thought.

Peter wrinkled up his nose. "Not much. A little more than you do, I'd say!"

"How do you know I dislike her?" Anna asked solemnly.

"Don't you?" he said.

She thought about it. She thought about Wendy's flat features and the beautiful way she made up her eyes, eyes which otherwise were not in the least remarkable. In fairness, she had to admit that Wendy certainly made the best of herself. Her clothes were always immaculate, if not very well chosen for messing about in boats and if she disliked Peter, at least she was honest about it. Many girls would have pretended a fondness at least until after they had got Piran's ring on their finger.

"She isn't my type," she said aloud to Peter.

"She isn't mine either," he said with engaging candour. "In fact I can't stand her. It's funny really, for Mike says she is a man's woman. He likes her well enough."

"Does he, though?" Anna was intrigued. Not in the fact that Michael should like Wendy; it would be more extraordinary if he didn't try his hand with every woman he came across, but she couldn't help feeling that it would be contrary to his interests for Wendy to fall in love with anyone but Piran. She was surprised that Michael Vaynor should have tried to divert Wendy's attention to himself, though. It showed a stupid streak that she hadn't thought was there. "How well?"

Peter looked embarrassed. "I don't know. Michael's a bit strange about some things."

"And Piran isn't?" Anna suggested with a smile.

"No," Peter agreed, with something very like wonder in his voice. "No, he's not. I hadn't thought about it before." He sounded quite worried, as if it really mattered to him. "Do you think my mother could have been like Michael?" he asked.

Anna shook her head. "I don't know," she said. "I didn't know her."

Peter coloured uneasily. "I think she may have been. I don't mean she was disloyal or anything like that, but I don't think she found it enough to be here with us all the time. That doesn't make her bad, does it?"

"No, of course not!" Anna agreed firmly.

She turned her head to see how far Wendy and Piran had progressed up the path to the fishermen's cabins at the top. They were nowhere in sight. She blinked once or twice, expecting to see them reappear again with the fish, but they did not. In an agony she wondered what they could be doing. She had not long to wait for an answer. They came from behind the shacks, their hands linked, smiling at one another. It was easy to see that they had been kissing – how, Anna didn't know. It was something in the zest with which they walked, something in the way they looked at one another. They looked, she thought, like any other couple in love.

She would have liked to have gone inside the cabin and shut the door, as a gesture that would cut out Piran Trethowyn from her life once and for all. But it would take more than a gesture to remove the pain she felt – she would not admit that it was jealousy – and anyway, she hoped she had more dignity than to allow any of them to see that she was hurt. Instead she forced herself to watch them gather up the wooden boxes of fish and their slow descent. She wouldn't help them, not she! She wouldn't lift a finger to help them bring the fish on board! Peter would have to do it!

Piran ran down the slipway, his hair lifting in the wind, a

broad smile on his face. "Quick!" he shouted at them. "Hurry up! The seals are sunning themselves on the rocks on the other side of the point. If we slip round under sail we'll get a really good view of them!"

He threw the box of gleaming mackerel on board and turned back to take Wendy's box from her, jumping on board with it in his hands. Peter tried to haul up the sail by himself, but it was too heavy for him. Piran tersely ordered Anna to help him, while he busied himself with bringing Wendy back on board. Anna thought her shining face was the last straw, but she said nothing. It was a relief to have something to do, something that taxed her physical strength to the limit, for she found lifting the sails extremely hard work.

Peter crowed delightedly as the wind caught at the canvas and sent them scudding out of Prussia Cove into the open sea. Even Wendy seemed tense with excitement and anticipation; she could have been a different person from her former sea-sick self cowering in the cabin. Only Anna could find little to get excited about, or so she thought. But as they rounded the point and the little grey, old-men faces of the seals appeared beside them in the water, she became as keen as they were. The seals showed no sign of being afraid of the boat. They flopped in and out of the water, some of them basking lazily on the flat-topped rocks, others playing in the water, diving and rising again, with one or two flipping an occasional fish into the air and demolishing it with a single gulp.

Peter kept the sloop as close in as he dared until the rumble of a passing boat scattered the seals into the water, only to return again as an ancient fishing boat made its stately way home to St. Michael's Mount.

"Aren't they sweet!" Wendy exclaimed, referring to the seals. "I wonder if they know they're a tourist attraction?"

"Probably," Piran smiled. "There are boats that come out

102

of Penzance several times a week in the summer."

"They strike me as being too shy to line up to have their photographs taken," Anna protested. They were too shy to come near the boat once they had seen it, she noticed. They kept well away from any real contact with their human admirers.

"You could be right," Piran agreed. He issued a brief command to Peter to alter course and they swung out to sea and the deeper waters of the Channel outside and away from Mount's Bay.

Anna sat on a stool in the cockpit beside Peter, watching everything that went on. Every now and then she had to duck her head as they went about and the boom passed over her head. Piran had taken Wendy forward to try to hoist the spinnaker, a gorgeous, peppermint-striped affair, that contrasted oddly with the rust red of the sails. It proved to be a fiddly operation before they could get it just right. At intervals, Ann could hear Wendy's whoops of delight as the foamy water streaked away beneath her, and she tried to prevent herself from hoping the other girl would fall in.

"She doesn't seem to be seasick now!" she commented to Peter, ashamed of herself even as she said the words.

Peter grinned. "Wait until we get out in the Channel. It can get pretty choppy out there."

They looked at each other and laughed.

"What beasts we are!" Anna grinned.

"Women shouldn't be on boats in the first place!" Peter retorted.

"Why not? Do you believe we're unlucky?" Anna asked him, mildly amused that he should be so vehement.

Peter chuckled. There was no doubt about it, he was quite definitely moving his feet to brace himself the better every time he brought the boat about, Anna observed. It would probably be a mistake to tell him so, though, until he discovered it for himself. "Some women are more unlucky than others," he told her.

She found herself laughing as well. "I believe you're jealous of Piran!" she teased him.

"Isn't that the pot calling the kettle black?" he returned.

"No," she denied harshly. "You ought to be jealous for him. He isn't just an acquaintance that you happened to meet one day."

"No, he's not," the boy agreed. "It's funny, because it would suit me very well if he did marry Wendy. I'd be able to go to London then, wouldn't I? *She* wouldn't want me!"

"But you don't want him to marry her?" Anna suggested gently.

The boy sighed. "No," he said reluctantly.

They knew immediately when they had left the sheltering arms of Mount's Bay. The rolling motion of the boat became more pronounced and the sea, which in the Bay was emerald green and sometimes navy blue, was now almost black.

"Hey, you two!" Peter shouted out. "How about trying our luck here?"

Piran jumped to his feet, studying the water around the boat carefully. "Right!" he called back. "I'll let go the drag anchor. Wendy, pull in the spinnaker! Anna, get those sails down!"

Anna had Peter's help, but even so she prided herself that she had not made such a mess of the sails as Wendy had of the spinnaker. She practically turned it inside out, before she could get it unhooked. It trailed pathetically in the water, first as a sodden ball of coloured canvas, then slowly stretching itself out in a streamer beside the boat.

"I can't help it!" Wendy said crossly. "I don't know how to undo the beastly thing!"

Both the Trethowyns were furious at the display of lack of

seamanship. Peter ground his teeth helplessly from his seat. "What did I tell you?" he said to Anna. "Just look at it!"

But to Anna, Piran's anger was the more menacing of the two. With a speaking glance at the unfortunate Wendy, he advised her to go aft with the others, so politely that even Anna shivered at the tone in his voice. Then, with truly magnificent patience, he hauled the spinnaker in from the water, folding it neatly and stowing it away in the forward locker.

"I hate boats!" Wendy said sulkily.

"Then you shouldn't go on them!" Piran told her silkily.

The sloop shuddered to a stop as the drag anchor stopped her drifting. Without the sails up there seemed to be suddenly more room for everyone. Up above them the sun beat down mercilessly on to the decks and sea.

"It'll rain before we get in," Peter told them.

Piran sniffed at the wind. "You could be right," he said.

Wendy went white. "Do you mean we're going to have a storm as well as everything else?" she demanded.

The men shrugged their shoulders, smiling faintly at a joke that was all their own. "I shouldn't think so," Piran answered. "Nothing to worry about, anyway."

He began opening up all the lockers in the cockpit, pulling out the fishing tackle that had been stowed away there after the last time he and Peter had gone out fishing together. With well-skilled hands, he tested the tension of the rods thoughtfully.

"I think this one will do for you," he said to Anna. "Try it out."

Anna had never so much as held a fishing rod in her hand before. She eyed the massive hooks with distaste, though she had to admire the workmanship that had gone into the steel-hearted rod. It whipped back and forth at a touch and was incredibly light in her hands.

"The line has an eighty-pound breaking strain," Piran told

her. "You want to look out that the shark doesn't get away by fouling up your line. He weighs rather more than eighty pounds," he added with a grin.

Anna rather hoped that the sharks would have too much sense to test her capabilities. She didn't think she would enjoy playing a sardine on the end of a line, let alone a monster that had real teeth with which to snap at her and anything else that came within range.

Wendy refused to take a rod at all. She would, she said, prepare some food for them all inside the cabin. She made it sound as if she were too sensitive and feminine to do battle with anyone, Anna thought with a grimace. She had an idea that Wendy was not nearly so sensitive when it came to people, especially those of her own sex.

Piran pulled out the bucket of rubby-dubby and mashed it up even more with a booted foot. The smell was horrible.

"That should draw them," he said with satisfaction.

"Certainly should!" the boy agreed, holding his nose. "Chuck it overboard, quick!"

His father did so, handful by handful, watching the mushy, smelly fish sink slowly beneath the surface. When he had finished laying the trail, he washed his hands in the sea, playing with the water as he scooped it up and allowed it to trickle away through his fingers.

"All we have to do now is to wait," he said.

Peter tested his rod carefully. He alone wore a harness with a socket into which he could fit his rod. It helped him to keep his balance when he had a bite, leaving his hands and forearms free to play the fish, without having to take the whole strain as well. He had only just fitted the rod into its socket when the first black dorsal fin could be seen hurrying towards the boat. Piran baited his hook with a couple of mackerel and trailed his line over the side of the boat.

106

Anna looked at the gleaming mackerel and then at her hook. "Could you bait it for me?" she asked in a tremulous voice.

He smiled quite gently at her. "It used to do things to my susceptibilities too," he admitted. "You get used to it."

"Blunted?" Peter suggested sweetly, one eye on Wendy in the cabin.

Piran chuckled. "You never had much to blunt!" he retorted. He arranged the mackerel neatly so that they completely hid the double hook and returned the line to Anna. "Try that," he said.

She felt quite professional once she had cast her line. The reel came under her right hand and it was instinct that showed her how to let the line out and how to reel it in again. She even liked the sound that it made, winding and unwinding in the still air. If this was fishing, she liked it after all, she decided. It was a peaceful, placid occupation, with just enough to do to keep one from getting bored. She had a look at what Piran was doing, trying to follow his every action in case she did the wrong thing. In fact, so intent was she on *his* line, and *his* rod, that she failed to see the large black shape of a shark as it slipped round the stern of the boat. The first she knew was a tremendous pull on her line that nearly jerked her arms out of her shoulders. It was the pain in her muscles, pain such as she had never felt before, that gave her that touch of temper to make her fight. "All right!" she said aloud. "*You're on!* If that's what you want!"

"Let the line out!" Piran shouted at her. She could see out of the corner of her eye how he longed to wrench the rod away from her, but nobody was going to interfere with her shark! *Nobody!*

"What do I do now?" she cried.

"Play it! Make it fight itself! Mind you don't fall in with it!"

She let the line out as far as it would go. It was a strange sensation to feel the weight of the shark pulling against her. She soon learned the art of playing the giant fish, rather as one might use judo, using the momentum of one's adversary to one's own advantage. For half an hour she battled with her catch. Her arms ached and so did every bone in her body. She had to concentrate every moment in case the shark made a sudden dash for freedom and caught her unawares. But at last she was able to draw it in beside the boat and she could see its great snapping jaws and its tail churning up the water until it foamed white all round it.

"Gaff!" Piran ordered suddenly. "Give me a gaff!"

Peter reached forward and handed it to him. "Will you need another?" he asked.

Piran had no breath to answer. A mere nod of the head was all he could manage. "Can you help?" he breathed.

The boy leaned as far forward as he could, catching at the shark's gills with the gaff in his hand. "Gently, or we'll lose it. Wind in, Anna!"

His excitement was contagious. The strain on her arms made her whole body tremble, but she kept her grip until the last. Then, suddenly, the whole thing was over. Piran caught the shark squarely with the gaff and hauled it over the side into the cockpit beside them. Anna leapt back, away from the violent spasms of the great fish as it lashed out. It was an evil-looking beast, saved only by the grandeur of its size from being totally repellent. Piran killed it quickly and efficiently and she felt nothing at all. She had seen now the way its great jaws could snap a living fish in two; it was not for nothing that the shark is known as the scourge of the deep.

"They'll smell blood over a mile away," Piran told her.

Peter laughed at the look on her face. "You're quite safe," he teased her. "They prefer male flesh to female any day of the week!'"

But Anna preferred not to make the experiment.

When the shark was still, Piran hung it from the masthead. It was only a few inches shorter than Anna was herself.

"It's quite big, isn't it?" she said conversationally, longing to be congratulated on what she thought was a splendid effort on her part.

"It's a big 'un," Piran agreed.

"It's huge!" Anna reproved him.

He considered it thoughtfully. "It's not the biggest I've ever seen," he said.

"It's the biggest *I've* ever seen!" Anna assured him.

Piran laughed at her. "Have you seen many?" he asked her slyly.

She shook her head, joining in the laughter. "I've seen them on television often enough," she excused herself. "And *that one* –" she pointed to her catch – "is a monster!"

"It deserves some kind of celebration," Peter agreed judiciously. "Shall we call in at St. Michael's Mount on the way home and have a pasty?"

"What?" his father exclaimed. "Not champagne?"

"I don't think the café runs to it," Peter said seriously. "We'd have to go somewhere else for that."

But St. Michael's Mount was nearer than Penzance and they were all hungry now that the battle was over. Piran cleared up the mess in the cockpit, swabbed down the decks to removed the last of the smell of the rubby-dubby, pausing now and then to admire Anna's shark.

"We'll weigh it when we get back to Penzance," he promised her.

Anna thanked him prettily. But now that it was all over, she felt as if she had been trampled on. Her muscles had already stiffened in the breeze that had come up from no-

where, bringing some thick black clouds with it, now no bigger than a man's hand, but soon to grow into a ridge of rain
clouds. She sat on the floor of the cockpit, watching Peter as
he set the compass and Piran as he hauled up the sails single-
handed, for Wendy was still in the cabin.

"We could do with something hot to drink!" Peter sang
out, as the wind hit the canvas. "Piran, I'll hold her on course
if you can raise the drag-anchor."

His father pulled the anchor on board with a grunt. He was
tired as well. On his way back to the cockpit he slapped his
hand down on the top of the cabin.

"What's the matter, Wendy? Have you gone to sleep, or
something?"

Wendy emerged slowly from the cabin. "I don't see why I
should have to make the tea," she said. "*I* didn't have the fun!"

"I'll get it," Anna offered. "I can't complain that I didn't
have any fun. You may have wielded the gaff," she added to
Piran, "but I consider that to be *my* fish!"

Peter grinned. "I wielded a gaff too!" he reminded her.

She stuck her tongue out at him. "I knew you Trethowyns
would take all the credit!" she said with dignity.

"Well, I'm blowed!" Piran exclaimed. "We might, if Anna
St. James wasn't so busy crowing about her triumph!"

Anna laughed. She was still smiling when she went inside
the cabin and put the kettle on to boil. Through the portholes
she could see the clouds rushing across the sky towards them.
She shivered, pulling her sweater closer about her. If they
didn't beat the weather, it was going to be rough, she thought.

When the kettle had boiled, she filled up the mugs with the
scalding hot tea and went back up on deck. She gave Wendy
an anxious look, but the other girl showed no signs of her
earlier seasickness. On the contrary, she was busy making up
her face, carefully outlining her eyes.

110

"I think we'd better use the engine as well," Piran said. "We don't want Anna's shark to get wet!"

Peter nodded. He started the engine easily and pushed the gear-leaver forward. Behind them the propellor roared into action and they cut through the waves as easily as a knife through butter.

St. Michael's Mount became clearly visible a few minutes later. Now that the clouds had blotted out the sun, it looked less golden but just as solid as ever. Soon it was possible to make out the individual houses of Marazion too, as they came right into Mount's Bay and ran for the shelter of the harbour of St. Michael's Mount, facing the beach of the small town from where one could walk to and fro across the causeway at low tide.

The harbour was bigger than Anna had expected. It had a remarkably wide entrance which some people say is because it was from here that the Phoenicians of old loaded up their ships with the precious Cornish tin. Peter steered them straight through the middle of the high, embracing walls and brought them in neatly beside some granite steps that led up to the top. Here, at high tide, several boats landed sightseers from Marazion, but there were none there now, for a light drizzle had already started, threatening heavy rain within the hour.

Wendy went up the steps first, with Anna close behind her. At the top was a tiny brass footprint, marking the spot where Queen Victoria had once stepped ashore many years before on a visit to the Mount.

"Run!" Piran bade her. "You'll get wet if you linger. Run straight on! The café's on your left."

But Wendy refused to hurry. She waited for Piran to step ashore and then she reached up and kissed him on the cheek. "That's for being nice to Anna," she said.

Piran's eyes met Anna's. There was no confusion, nothing

111

that she could see within them. Anna bit her lip and turned away. It had been her shark, she thought bitterly, but the victory belonged to Wendy. It was she, by not even trying, who had gained Piran's approval in the end. For many days to come it would be very hard to forgive her that.

CHAPTER EIGHT

THE rain was short and sharp. It splattered down, bouncing off the ground and water alike. In ten minutes, however, it was over and the sun broke through the low bank of cloud and cast a watery gleam across the Mount. Piran managed to ease Peter's wheelchair out of the shop where they had taken shelter, while the two girls finished buying some of the postcards and fascinating souvenirs that were on sale.

More interesting than the guide books, picture match boxes, and other odds and ends, Anna found the stuffed animals and the other remnants of what had once been a museum intriguing. But once the rain had gone, there was no time to linger. They were all far too hungry not to press on to the café.

The Cornish pasties were hot and sustaining. Anna bit into hers carefully, afraid that it would crumble in her hands, but it showed no signs of doing so. It was a satisfying experience, she discovered, to eat a whole meal encased in pastry. It was easy, convenient, and very welcome. The café, too, appealed to her. She liked the old granite millstones that had been turned into tables, set out in the small grassy enclosure that looked out to Marazion across the old battlements where, probably, once guns had stood.

The café was empty except for themselves. They sat on rain-spattered chairs, refusing to go inside, and Piran told them some of the local fishing stories and about the mermaids who had once, apparently, run wild in the little coves all round the coast. They had almost finished eating when he suddenly looked at Peter and said, in a off-hand way, as if he didn't care one way or the other, "Care to come to London with me one day next week?"

The boy flushed. "Really? Do you mean it?"

Piran nodded indifferently. "It's time you went back to the hospital anyway."

Peter went as white as before he had been scarlet. "Is that all?"

"What did you think?" Piran mocked him.

"I thought – I thought you meant we'd have *fun*!" the boy stammered.

"Isn't it possible to do both?" his father asked him.

"Not with you!" Peter said rudely. "I know exactly how it will be. You'll take me to the hospital, and you won't even come and see me –"

"That isn't what I said," Piran cut him off. "I only want you to see the specialist. We can take in dinner and a show as well if you like?"

"I don't like!" Peter sulked.

Anna sat up very straight. She blinked rapidly, secretly appalled that she was going to interfere in what was strictly a Trethowyn affair once again.

"But you *must* see the specialist!" she burst out. "Peter, we saw you on the boat! *You moved your legs!*"

He smiled fleetingly at her. "That for a yarn!" But she could see that he would have liked to have believed her.

"Who told you you would never walk again?" she asked him sternly.

"Uncle Mike –" The boy broke off, casting a sulky look at his father. "I knew all along. *You* couldn't bear to see me after the crash, could you? But he came, often!"

Piran made no attempt to defend himself. He clenched his fists and looked at his son. "We're going to London next week whether you like it or not. Understand?"

Peter turned his chair so that he didn't have to look at his father. "It's always been the same!" he said bitterly.

"It isn't the same at all!" Anna contradicted him flatly. "How can walking be the same as being confined to a wheel-chair?"

Wendy made a little exclamation of shock. "How can you?" she muttered. "Why do you have to remind him?"

"Why not?" Peter drawled. His face was still very white.

"Because you're such a fool!" Anna told him, exasperated. "Why, this might have happened years ago if you'd done your exercises properly, but you wouldn't! And now, when you are doing them and *they've done you some good*, you won't even believe it!"

Piran grinned. "Downright cussed of you!" he said with a laugh.

"It's easy for you!" Peter stormed back, ignoring his father. "You didn't have to go through it all!"

"No," Anna admitted. "But I watched my mother go through quite a lot. I'm pleased to say," she added, "that the St. Jameses seem to have more stamina than the Treth-owyns –"

"That's too much!" Wendy protested. "That's a *cheap* thing to say –"

"Oh, shut up!" Peter snapped. "Can't you see she's trying to make me angry?"

'Do I have to try?" Anna asked him pointedly.

"No. I'm angry all right!" He smiled with genuine amusement, his eyes lighting up. "At least, I *was* angry. But you needn't think the St. Jameses are better than the Trethowyns in any way. I don't think it will do any good, but I'll see the the specialist – for you!"

"For your father," Anna pleaded with him.

The sulky frown came back to his face. "For you!" he said flatly.

115

Anna could have wept. She didn't dare look at Piran in case he thought that she had wanted Peter to hurt him, though why he should think anything of the sort was more than she could say.

"Perhaps Anna had better come with us?" Piran drawled.

"No!" The single expletive was met with silence. Anna moved restively on her chair. "I don't want to," she added. "I'd be in the way."

"Perhaps," Piran agreed. He stood up with a brief suggestion that they should go back to the boat and strode off, ahead of them, leaving them to follow as best they could. Wendy ran after him, clucking sympathetically, winding her arm into his. He gave her an affectionate hug and they walked on together.

Anna pushed Peter to the top of the steps on the harbour wall with a violence that brought a brooding protest from the boy.

"Look," he said, "Michael told me the truth years ago. There's no chance of my walking again. That's why Piran never contested my mother's will. He thought I'd need the money."

"Then how come you were using your legs in the boat?" Anna demanded.

Peter fell silent. "I don't know," he said eventually.

Wendy had already gone on board when Anna and Peter got to the top of the steps. Anna stood by while Piran lifted the boy on to the boat. He ran lightly up the steps again and passed the folded chair to her to stow away in the cabin.

"Anna," he said urgently.

She looked back up at him over her shoulder. "Yes?"

"You can't come with us," he said flatly. "Someone has to keep an eye on Michael."

She very nearly missed her footing and took a header into

116

the harbour.

"Why?" she asked.

He smiled at her so sweetly that her heart turned over. "You'll know why, when you think about it. Please, Anna?"

She pushed the folded chair on to the boat ahead of her. "Okay," she said. "If you'll look after Peter every moment of time while you're away?"

"It's a bargain!" he said.

Anna was agreeably surprised by the size of the cheques she was beginning to receive from the London stores.

"If only I were any good at figures!" she said to Ellen. "At the moment, I feel positively rich. But I suppose I ought to keep a good half of the money for taxes?"

"I couldn't say, dearie," Ellen replied. "It sounds a great deal," she added with respect, "but I haven't any head for business. It's the boy you should be asking. He has no difficulty with figures."

"But I can hardly burden him with my finances!" Anna objected.

"Why not?" Ellen retorted. "It'll take his mind off going up to London with his father, and that would be a kindness for us all!"

Peter proved to be only too willing to work out Anna's tax situation. He sat in the hearth, surrounded by cheques, receipts, and a handy tax reckoner, and set to work with a will.

"You couldn't possibly need to keep *half*!" he had said to Anna grandly. "I don't suppose you even pay surtax?"

"I should hope not!" Anna had replied, horrified.

"I do," he had told her with a touch of pride. "At least, I think it's added on to Piran's income. He actually pays it."

Anna had thought nothing of it at the time. She had left Peter to struggle with her earnings, while she had gone into

117

the other room to fetch the fine, silver wire that she was using to join some pretty coloured pebbles together into a necklace. It was only when she came back that she thought to ask:

"I suppose you pay surtax on the money your mother left you?"

Peter threw down his pen, pleased to have caught her attention so successfully. "Yes," he said. "Piran will never tell me exactly how much it is, but it's quite safe! I'll get it when I'm eighteen. Meanwhile, there's some kind of a trust that's supposed to pay for my needs, only Piran won't touch a penny of it."

Anna sat down thoughtfully. "It seems odd to me," she said. "Your uncle doesn't seem to be very well off."

Peter laughed. "He isn't!" he disclaimed. "Mike never has any money. He's always borrowing from his friends. It makes Piran crosser than anything! And that makes it funny, if you know what I mean?"

"Not exactly," Anna said gently. "How did your mother come to have so much money when her brother has so little?"

"It's Trethowyn money," Peter explained.

"No, I don't understand at all –" Anna said, bewildered.

"Well, it's silly really," the boy admitted. "You see, Piran was brought up by his grandparents. His mother lived here too, of course, but she didn't count. It was his grandfather that mattered. He was rich enough, but so mean that he made things unbearable for everyone. But when he died, he left all his money to his wife. It caused endless gossip because it wasn't what anyone had expected him to do and people said she'd brought pressure on him as he lay on his death bed. I don't think anyone really cared if she had, though. Well, *she* was so tired of being kept short of money that she spent an awful lot, and she refused to leave what was left to Piran, because she thought all men were tarred with the same brush.

So she left the money to my mother instead. It was really *for* Piran, but so that he couldn't keep his wife as short of money as his grandfather had kept her."

"And your mother left the money to you?"

The boy nodded. "It was a joke to annoy Piran. Wendy suggested it. She kept on and on telling my mother that Piran didn't want either of us. They were rather friendly," he went on awkwardly. "My mother never saw that Wendy was only using her. She was a bit silly, but she was *nice*, if you know what I mean." He paused, wrapped up in his own memories of his mother. "She wouldn't have kept the money," he said finally. "She would have given it back to him, and have changed the will and everything, as soon as she got her divorce. But she was killed first."

"Poor woman!" Anna remarked. "And poor Piran!"

The boy clenched his teeth. "I don't see why. He could have contested the will if he'd wanted to."

"Whereas Mr. Vaynor could take the lot without lifting a finger, if he had you to live with him," Anna suggested innocently.

"But he isn't like that!" Peter protested. "How can you say such a thing?"

"I didn't," Anna told him. "He did. He said the money was Vaynor money and really his."

Peter was silent for a long moment. "I don't believe you," he said then. "He – he isn't like that! He wouldn't mind scoring off Piran, but the money is Trethowyn money. He knows that!"

"Piran seems to think it's your money rather than belonging to the Trethowyns," Anna put in.

Peter looked puzzled. "What's the difference?" he said.

"I don't know," Anna admitted. "But I think he works pretty hard for his money. He does all that tourist business and so on for the county, and then there's the mead business –"

"He didn't have that before my mother died," Peter told her. "Mr. Morris owned it and then Wendy wanted him to go in with her when her father pulled out. He said he had to because Wendy had been such a good friend to my mother. It's only just beginning to pay. He had far more money before – all this happened."

"I expect he did," Anna said gently. "But afterwards your mother's money would be tied up, wouldn't it? First probate would have to be granted and then it was your money. He couldn't use *that* money to finance the mead business, could he?"

"He could have contested the will," Peter said again. "I would have done!"

"Then why don't you ask him why he didn't?" Anna suggested.

"Perhaps I will," Peter said thoughtfully.

It would be a mistake to press him, Anna thought. She hoped it would occur to him that if Piran had had little or no money after his wife's death, there was a reason why he had left Peter in London, in the hospital by himself.

"You know," Peter went on, "I wouldn't mind if you were to marry Piran. I like you better than Wendy, and besides, you don't talk down to me."

"I should hope not!" Anna exclaimed.

"Some people do," he said. "If you were to marry Piran, would you live here?"

Anna gave herself a little shake. "He wouldn't want to marry me, so the question doesn't arise," she said sternly.

"But if he did?" Peter insisted.

There was no harm in dreaming, Anna supposed. She sat back in her chair and tried to imagine what it would be like to be married to Piran. The thought made her tremble inside.

She wouldn't admit, even to herself, that she was in love with him. Why should she? He wasn't at all what she wanted in a husband. She wanted a man who was all her own; who was charming and strong; someone to sweep her off her feet; a dream lover such as all young girls imagine at one time or another. And Piran wasn't at all like that. He could be charming, but he was just as often sulky and silent. Nor could he ever belong only to her, for he had been married before, whether she liked it or not, and the result of that marriage was Peter. But she loved Peter. That surprised her. She had known that she *liked* the boy right from the beginning, but now she could hardly imagine life without him.

She stared at him as though she had never seen him before, shaken more by this discovery than she had been by the insidious discovery that she was in love with Piran.

"What's the matter?" Peter asked her.

She shook herself and cleared her throat. "Why, nothing!" she said fiercely. "What could be the matter?"

The boy shrugged. "You looked as if you'd just seen a ghost," he told her. "And you didn't say if you would live in Cornwall if you were married to Piran?"

"I — I suppose I would," she stammered. "I'd have to live in his home, wouldn't I?"

"If he married again —"

"He won't marry me!" she said with certainty.

"But," Peter insisted, "if he did, you wouldn't want me around, would you?"

"Why ever not?" Her voice trembled slightly, but she hoped he hadn't noticed.

The boy blushed. "Most women wouldn't want me."

"Rubbish!" Anna said vigorously. "I've never heard such nonsense! Any woman —"

"Not any woman," he contradicted her. He smiled slowly,

looking very pleased with himself. "It's nice to know you would have me," he said.

Anna looked shocked. "You talk a great deal of nonsense," she told him gruffly. "Have you worked out the tax yet?"

"Yes," he said. He rattled off a figure that sounded astronomical to her unaccustomed ears. "It isn't nearly as bad as *half*," he teased her.

"Isn't it?" she said vaguely. "It sounds a lot of money –"

He looked at her closely. "It isn't really," he said. "Didn't you make as much in London?"

"Nothing like!" she told him cheerfully. "Things seem to be getting better and better!"

Peter studied his fingers carefully. "When you were in London, you had to support your mother as well, didn't you?"

"What if I did?" she returned.

"I just wondered." He sounded suddenly shy. "Did you have enough –? I mean, could you buy her everything she needed?"

"I tried to," she said.

He pushed the papers together and handed them to her, the figures of what she had received and what she would have to pay all neatly marked on a separate sheet. "I'd better go now," he muttered. He began to wheel himself towards the door. "By the way," he said over his shoulder, "when we go to London, will you come and see us off?"

She was tremendously flattered. "If you want me to?" she said.

He grinned at her. "You would have come anyway," he teased her.

Would she have done? She couldn't say. "When you're walking again," she told him, "I'll treat you as you deserve!"

"When!" he grunted. It was easy to see that he didn't believe a word of it. Anna could only hope that the specialist would be able to convince him that he was wrong. She sighed,

122

saddened by the long, hard battle that she knew must lie ahead of him.

She went to the station, of course. The night train left for Paddington at ten o'clock in the evening, but travellers were allowed to board the train half an hour before. Anna took the bus into Penzance, walking the short distance between the bus stop, across where the taxis waited for fares, to the station yard and the platform where the train was standing.

Peter saw her at once. He wheeled his chair down the platform to meet her.

"So you did come!" he exclaimed.

"I thought you asked me to!" she retorted.

Piran came strolling over to join them. "He's been on tenterhooks all evening in case you didn't come," he told her, mildly amused.

She forced a rather awkward smile. "And you?" she challenged him.

"I *knew* you'd come," he claimed.

"I don't see how you could?" she answered, puzzled.

"No, perhaps you wouldn't," he agreed. "One day I'll tell you why – if you promise not to hold it against me!"

"I won't!" she promised happily. There was something in his eyes that gave a lift to her spirits and she was doubly glad that she had come.

"Why don't you get on?" Piran suggested to Peter. "I'll come and see that you're comfortable and then I'll have a word with Anna. I have something to say to her."

"Something private?" the boy asked him resentfully.

Piran grinned at him. "Something about you, of course!" he said mildly.

Peter smiled reluctantly. "That's dampened my curiosity!" he admitted. He leaned forward in his chair. "But remember,

123

Anna is a nice girl! She wouldn't understand the things that make the Trethowyns tick!"

"Speak for yourself!" his father retorted.

Anna, aware of them both looking at her, could feel herself blushing. "I don't know what you're talking about," she said.

"Exactly!" they chimed in together.

Peter wheeled his chair close to her and, very much to her surprise, offered his face for her farewell kiss. With a rush of affection for him, she made a motion towards him, careful not to seem too eager or too sentimental.

"I'll expect you to come back walking," she said lightly.

"Well, I won't be," he answered gruffly, "it will be enough if there really is some kind of movement. But I doubt it!" He smiled up at his father in a way Anna had never seen him do before. "I think you're both a great deal too eager for it to be true! You probably imagined it."

Anna shook her head. "I'm sure we didn't," she said simply.

Piran signalled to the sleepng car attendant to help him and between them they lifted Peter on to the train and settled him on the lower bunk in their compartment. Anna waved to him through the window and he waved back at her.

"Has he got anything to read?" she asked Piran when he stepped down on to the platform again.

"A couple of paperbacks, I think. He probably ought to have some of his school work with him too, but I doubt that he brought any of that!"

Anna laughed. "Oh well," she said, "the idea is that you should enjoy yourselves — together, isn't it?"

"It is." He hesitated. "I have an idea that I have to thank you for a lot," he said awkwardly.

She could feel herself blushing again. "I *like* Peter," she told him.

He smiled. "I rather think he returns the compliment," he

124

said. "If so, you're the first woman he has ever been able to tolerate!"

She shook her head. "That's not true! He was devoted to his mother —"

"She didn't treat him very well," Piran said wryly.

"Perhaps that doesn't always matter very much," she suggested gently.

He looked at her closely. "I believe you'd have a kind word for anyone," he said.

She felt a hypocrite, for she knew how far from the truth that was. She had only to think about Wendy, for instance, for all her better nature to desert her with a rush.

"I — I think I'd better go and let you get back to Peter," she said hurriedly. "It won't be long before the train goes."

He put out a hand to stop her. "I must speak to you first. Anna, will you do something for me?"

She looked him straight in the face. "Yes," she said. She could feel the grip of his fingers through her light coat. With half of her, she resented the arrogance of his touch; the other half tingled with sheer delight.

"It's about Michael —"

She froze. "What about him?" she asked, her voice hoarse.

He eyed her quizzically. "I wish I knew how you really felt about him," he said softly. "But I have to ask you this —"

"Oh?" She had meant to sound dignified; in fact she sounded downright haughty.

"This is the first chance I've had of reaching Peter since the accident," he pleaded with her. "I don't want Michael to spoil it. Do you think you could try to keep him away from London for the next two days?"

"Me?" she said, astonished. "He won't pay any attention to me!"

125

"He might," Piran said grimly. "It depends what you say to him."

"What do you mean?" Anna was aware of a sinking feeling in her middle. She wanted nothing to do with Michael Vynor! She feared him in a way that she didn't understand.

"He'll only come to London if he knows why Peter and I have gone there," Piran told her certainly. "Can you keep the information from him until I get back?"

"Doesn't he already know?" Ann wondered.

"Who would tell him?'

Anna wriggled uncomfortably. "Ellen," she said. "Or Wendy. Anyone might!"

Piran shook his head. "Ellen has her orders," he insisted, "and Wendy never sees him now." His face softened. "She's a loyal person and she knows what he's done to box things up for me."

Anna swallowed. It wasn't quite the impression she had received, but she supposed she might well be wrong. "I don't suppose I shall see him," she said. "I certainly shan't tell him where you are. I – I wouldn't anyway," she went on. "You see, I don't think he's very good for Peter."

Piran smiled at her. "Nor do I," he said.

She smiled uncertainly back. "You didn't have to ask, you know," she told him.

"No?"

She shook her head. "No," she said certainly.

His eyes glinted with mischief. "Not even for a kiss?" he asked her. "Shall I give you my payment in advance?"

"I – I don't know what you mean!"

He drew her into the circle of his arms, still smiling at her. "I think you do," he said. She could feel his breath in her hair and then on her brow. She made an agitated movement, but he paid no attention to her at all. "As a matter of fact," he said

126

in her ear, "I rather enjoy it myself!"

She would have given anything to have been able to produce just the right answer, but nothing occurred to her. It was humiliating but true that she did nothing more than stand there, with his arms about her, in an agony of anticipation. He was going to kiss her! She ought to object, of course. She ought to do something. But she did nothing – absolutely nothing!

He kissed her very gently on the lips. She shut her eyes, wondering why it should be that one man should have such an effect on her. There were so many nicer. less involved men for her to fall in love with, so why choose this one?

"I'm sorry, my darling, I shall have to go," he said at last.

Anna made no attempt to prevent him. He kissed her again on the cheek and laughed with sheer masculine triumph. "Very nice too!" he said. "What a good thing it is that we *like* the same things, don't you think?" he taunted her. He laughed again. "You needn't worry, I'll be quite sure to give your regards to Miss Bryant!"

"You dare!" she whispered. She watched him jump on the train through a mist of tears and the train began to slowly pull out of the station taking Piran with it. If it had not been for the pounding of her heart, his kiss might never have happened to her.

CHAPTER NINE

ANNA thought it would be a good opportunity to tidy up the cottage. No matter how careful she was, the dust from her pebbles and semi-precious stones got everywhere. She had dust sheets that she put down over all the furniture when she was working, but even so, every now and then she found it necessary to turn the whole place upside down. It had another advantage in that it inspired her to sort out all the pebbles she had collected into their various types. It was probably the only time that she really knew what she had.

To make things easier, Ellen willingly lent her the vacuum cleaner from the Trethowyn house. "My," she said, as she brought it over, "you won't know yourself when you've done, will you?"

Anna laughed. "It was getting pretty bad," she admitted. "I ought really to polish the stones outside, only the weather isn't always what one hopes it will be."

"That it's not!" Ellen agreed. "One day the sun bakes you alive and the next there's the mist to wrap you in a cold compress. Now, my handsome, you give me a call when you've done and I'll fetch the cleaner back myself. I'll not need it again today."

She didn't go immediately, though. Ellen liked a good gossip as well as anyone. "I'm going shopping," she announced after a while when the only answer she had raised from Anna was a series of grunts. "Is there anything that you want?"

Gratefully, Anna wrote her out a list. "Oh, and could you bring me back a pasty for lunch?" she added. "It doesn't look as though I'll have time for anything else!"

"You're a worker," Ellen said grudgingly. "I'll say that for you."

Anna smiled. "I have to be," she said. "I have to eat!"

Ellen shook her head wonderingly. "You're very different from Mrs. Trethowyn," she remarked.

"Which Mrs. Trethowyn?" Anna countered.

"I didn't know the old lady," Ellen told her. "A regular tartar she was, by all accounts. No, I was meaning Mrs. Caroline – Peter's mother."

"Didn't she work?" Anna asked.

Ellen sniffed. "Not so you'd notice! She was kind-hearted, mind, but she liked to have her own way."

Anna sighed. "Don't we all?" she said with feeling.

"Maybe," Ellen said darkly. "There's ways and ways of doing it, that's all I'm saying! Well," she added, seeing that she was not getting much response from Anna, "I'd better leave you to get on with it." She went to the door and looked out, smiling into the sunlight. "You won't be alone for long," she called over her shoulder. "You have a visitor coming!"

"Damn," said Anna.

"Now, Miss Anna," Ellen reproved her. "I'll be going," she went on hurriedly. "Miss Morris asks so many questions!"

Anna was startled to see Ellen sprinting across the grass to the big house. How odd, she thought, for she never would have supposed that Ellen would have forgone the chance of chatting with anyone.

Wendy didn't bother to knock. She stood in the doorway with all the poise of a fashion model, her clothes, and everything about her, immaculate. Anna looked from her to her shrouded room and giggled to herself. The contrast could not have been more obvious.

"Are you spring-cleaning, or what?" Wendy demanded.

"Come in," Anna greeted her as warmly as she could. "I
129

have to clear things up every now and again because I make such a mess with the grinders and polishers."

"So I see!" Wendy remarked. She ran her finger over the settle in the hearth, picked up a duster, cleaned a patch for herself and sat down, neatly crossing her legs.

Anna swallowed down the belligerent indignation that she seemed to feel whenever she saw Wendy, and attempted a smile. "Would you like some coffee?" she asked.

Wendy accepted the offer, her eyes flicking round Anna's few possessions, a slight smile on her face. "I came to see you about those bottles of yours," she said.

"Oh yes?" Anna answered cautiously.

"You see," Wendy went on, "Piran is away, so I'm in sole charge. I thought I might as well get the matter settled before he comes home."

Anna was genuinely surprised. "I thought it was settled," she said. "I thought you didn't want them?"

Wendy smiled carefully. "I never said that!" she retorted quickly. "I must admit I resented having them swung on me in that way, but I quite understood that you couldn't possibly have known how carefully Piran and I divide up our responsibility for the mead business. Even if he told you, you wouldn't have thought that it *mattered*!"

Anna was glad of the opportunity to leave the room to make the coffee. How dared Wendy Morris imply that it was she who had pushed the stone bottles on to Piran? She poured out the coffee, making it black and very strong. There was plenty of cream if Wendy wanted it and a selection of Cornish biscuits that came in rather a pretty tin embellished with Cornish symbols and the Cornish coat-of-arms.

"Can you turn out the bottles in any numbers?" Wendy asked her, as Anna came back into the room, carrying the tray.

"Not really," Anna told her. "They take rather a long time and, as you said before, they would be expensive for you to market."

Wendy's face flushed with temper. "I think you misunderstood me. They will be excellent as small gifts for people who have everything."

"Is that what Piran said?" Anna couldn't resist asking.

Wendy forced a smile. "I knew you'd say something like that," she said in forgiving tones. "I don't mind – you mustn't think I do! As a matter of fact, Piran has nothing to do with it." She fumbled in her handbag and drew out a piece of paper and a ballpoint pen. "Now, how much are your costs per bottle? I suppose you must have some idea?"

"I know exactly," Anna informed her quietly, too quietly.

"Really? Piran says you're an artist in your field, and you know what artists are like when it comes to money!"

"I know the cliché," Anna agreed.

Wendy didn't blink. "If you could bring your costs down to – say – fifty pence a bottle, that wouldn't be too bad! We could sell them for sixty pence each?"

"I can do that," Anna agreed.

"Of course, whether they'll go or not doesn't depend on me," Wendy went on brightly. "I can't guarantee anything."

"Nor can I," Anna said promptly. "I have rather a lot on hand at the moment. I can fit one or two in, but I have to meet my present commitments first and that takes up pretty well all my time."

Wendy didn't trouble to hide her disbelief. "It would be a good thing for you, Anna. We are *very* well known, and we would be generous about such things as credit for the design and so on."

"I still have to fulfil my present contracts first," Anna insisted doggedly.

"I didn't know you had any!" Wendy said in a wounded voice. "I do think I might have been told. I was under the impression that I was doing you a favour!"

"Oh?" Anna encouraged her.

"Well, it would help you, whatever you think!" Wendy pouted. "I had something I wanted to ask you too!"

"Ask away!" Anna invited her cheerfully.

"Yes, but you'd be much more inclined to help me if you were working for me, wouldn't you?"

Wendy looked so prettily distraught that Anna felt that she was being a beast to her. Besides, she was curious as to what Wendy could conceivably want of her.

"I might do it anyway," she joked.

Wendy's eyes narrowed. "You might! You know why Piran has taken Peter to London, don't you?"

Anna nodded. "What of it?"

"I want you to leave here while he's away!" Wendy burst out.

"But why?"

"He really thinks that Peter is getting better," Wendy explained. "And that's your fault, so I don't see why you shouldn't bear some of the consequences. If Peter ever were to walk again, Piran would get quite maudlin about him! As it is, they've never been able to get on. Piran can't stand seeing him wheeling himself around in that chair! It stands to reason, doesn't it? After all, *he* couldn't bring himself to wait around in London while Peter was recovering from the crash. Michael Vaynor had to do that!"

"Had to?" Anna raised her eyebrows and stared at Wendy.

"No one else was going to wet-nurse that horrid little boy! You have no idea what the scandal was like. My father broke under the strain —"

But you, Anna finished for her, took the opportunity to

prove your loyalty to Piran once and for all. But why? Was it only because she wanted to marry Piran herself?

"You don't like Peter, do you?" she said aloud.

Wendy suppressed a shudder. "It's wrong of me, I know, but it bothers me to see him – the way he is. I can't believe he couldn't stand up like everyone else and walk if he only wanted to. I have to keep looking at him to make sure that he isn't walking. I know he can't!" she added with a laugh. "I know he never will! But he's so like his mother. She was always there when one least wanted her to be, taking things that weren't hers!"

Anna coughed. She thought for an anxious moment that her coffee had gone down the wrong way, but she managed to retrieve the situation by taking a deep, gulping breath. "*What?*" she exclaimed.

Wendy's face became a complete blank. The flat planes of her cheeks, never her best feature, became tense and immobile. "She took Piran," she said with a hiss.

Acutely embarrassed, Anna chose to ignore this. "I thought Caroline was supposed to have been so like her brother?"

"In looks," Wendy admitted. "They're not at all alike in character."

Anna looked thoughtfully down at her hands. "And what would be gained by my going away?" she asked.

Wendy leaned forward eagerly. "Before you came, Michael was doing so well with the boy. He was the only one the little devil had any feeling for at all! Everything was working out so well. It would only have been a short time before Piran would have agreed to Mike's taking Peter away for ever. It wouldn't even have *hurt* him! He knew the boy didn't like him at all, so why should he have cared? Without that little cripple, he could have got on with his own life. We would have been happy at last –"

"We?" Anna interposed politely.

"Well, of course. He knows I'll only marry him if Peter goes away — for good. I intend to have my own family, not someone else's, ready made!"

"It can be awkward," Anna agreed.

"I was sure I could make you see my point of view," Wendy crowed in triumph. "Caroline was no more than an incident. She's dead now — dead and buried. The only thing of her left is the boy!" She clenched her fists. "I couldn't stand having him around, reminding me every minute of *her*!"

"And how does Piran feel?" Anna asked conversationally.

Wendy glanced at her uncomfortably. She was uneasily aware that she had said more than she meant to, and yet Anna seemed more sympathetic than she had supposed. Perhaps it didn't matter what she said, if only she could get her to go.

"We were engaged once," she answered in an unnatural voice.

"And then Caroline came along?" Anna said flatly.

Wendy nodded. "They were married almost at once. Everyone admired Caroline. They all went out of their way to tell me so. She was pretty, I suppose," she added disparagingly, "if you like that fair, overblown rose type. It wouldn't have lasted! She never took the least care of her looks."

"Michael is certainly handsome," Anna put in.

Wendy nodded abstractedly. "Men don't run to seed like women do," she muttered. "I kept telling Caroline that she hadn't as much time as she thought. She might have bowled Piran over when she first came back here, but it couldn't *last*. And it didn't," she went on smugly. "She was that sort of woman, you see. She would believe her friends sooner than her looking-glass. I don't think she ever understood why Piran had married her in the first place."

"Whereas you did?" Anna put in.

"He's mine!" Wendy went on with cool finality. "You might think you have Piran, I told her, but in the end he'll come back to me! Of course she tried to believe that it was her that he loved, but I soon scotched that. I liked her, you know. She was the only woman friend I've ever had. It was so *obvious* that Piran had no real feeling for her, and so I told her the truth."

Anna's lips felt stiff and her mouth dry. "Is that when she ran away?" she asked.

Wendy nodded, her eyes glittering. "She saw for herself that I was right! It's so undignified holding on to a man who has no feeling left for you, don't you think? At first she wasn't sure – Caroline hadn't much pride in herself. I told her she ought to get away while she could still find herself another man. She was quite pretty still and she didn't have any difficulty in attracting men."

"Wasn't that rather cruel of you?" Anna suggested.

Wendy shrugged. "She'd been cruel to me. She took Piran."

"And now I'm to go away?"

"Not far," Wendy said pacifically. "You'd feel much more at home in a place like St. Ives. There are lots of artistic people there!"

Anna nearly laughed. "I still don't see how my going would benefit you?" she said.

"You don't?" Wendy looked thoroughly pleased with herself. "I thought you were clever," she said naïvely. "I'm sure Piran told me you were." She gave Anna an odd look, which Anna returned with a blank stare. "Peter thinks you're absolutely marvellous," she rushed on, sure now of her audience. "You've given him such confidence! I'm sure you meant well, but if he were to become friends with Piran, he would hardly be willing to go and live with Michael, would he?"

"I don't think he really wants to anyway," Anna objected.

135

"But he *did*! He will again if you leave him to me –"

"Very likely," Anna agreed dryly. "How did you persuade Michael that he wanted Peter?"

"Oh, that wasn't difficult at all!" Wendy exclaimed. "Peter has all that money and Michael never has any at all!"

"Trethowyn money," Anna reminded her.

"What does it matter? The old lady was silly enough to leave it to Caroline and that made it Vaynor money, just as much as Trethowyn, didn't it? Anyway, Michael thinks so. And I have plenty of money of my own, so I didn't want it."

It was all so horrible that Anna could scarcely believe it. She thought of Caroline, badgered and frightened, running off with the first man who had come her way. And of Peter, small and unhappy, sure that he was unwanted by his father, and growing more and more withdrawn and bitter because of it. If before she had disliked Wendy, now she hated her.

"But Peter is going to walk," she said suddenly, with such complete certainty that she was a little surprised herself.

"He won't," Wendy contradicted, well pleased by the fact. "If he really believed he was able to, he might, but he won't otherwise. The doctor said so." She patted her immaculate hair-do and began to search in her handbag for her lipstick. "So that's settled, then? You'll go?"

Anna stood up slowly. "No," she said. "Nothing will move me out of this cottage until I see Peter on his feet and happy with his father. *Nothing!*"

Wendy finished making up her lips with a flourish. "Perhaps Michael will make you change your mind?" she said. "He's quite partial to you. Why don't you marry him, and then you'd have your precious Peter with you?"

But not Piran! some unbidden voice said within Anna. She was fond of Peter, very fond, but she *loved* Piran.

"Go away!" she said to Wendy. "Go away and take your

poison with you!"

Wendy laughed. "That's what you say now, but you won't stay you know. By the way," she added, "Michael is going up to London tonight, isn't that nice?"

Anna blenched. "You told him!" she exclaimed furiously.

"Of course. But Piran is going to think that you did," Wendy told her maliciously. "He won't be at all pleased, but I shall be here to comfort him." She walked across the room to the door, her high heels tapping against the floor. "Don't try to stop him, my dear," she advised. "He won't listen to you." She chuckled without any humour at all. "He's already sold out to me," she said.

Anna had cleaned every inch of the cottage by the time Ellen came back from Penzance with her shopping. The Cornish woman sniffed the air and eyed Anna's glum face sympathetically.

"She didn't stay long, then?" she inquired curiously.

"Long enough!" Anna said with feeling.

Ellen's eyes snapped with excitement. "Don't you like her, dearie?"

"No." Anna grasped the older woman by the shoulders and steered her into a seat. "Ellen, if I asked you some questions, would you tell me the truth?"

Ellen looked frightened. "Miss Anna, I –"

"Will you?" Anna insisted.

"Yes. Yes, I will. I wouldn't promise anything to anyone else, but you're good for the boy – good for Mr. Piran too."

Anna hesitated. If Piran knew that she was questioning his servants, he would be furious, and rightly so. But the mere thought of Wendy steeled her resolution. There was something truly evil about Wendy, something that had made her scrub

137

every inch of the cottage just to get rid of her lingering presence.

"Was Piran ever engaged to Wendy?" she brought out urgently.

Ellen nodded. "I don't know how serious it was. It didn't last a minute when he set eyes on Caroline, I know that much!"

"But he really was in love with Caroline?"

"He wouldn't have married her else," Ellen objected reasonably.

"But she ran away —"

"Ten years later! She and Miss Morris became quite good friends long before that."

"That's what I thought," Anna said slowly. "And I suppose Mr. Vaynor was always around too?"

"Not he! He came to the wedding, but he found Cornwall a great deal too dull for his tastes. It was only after the accident that he found himself a chalet to live in and settled in. He said it was to be near the boy." Ellen became quite perky for a minute. "It's always been a mystery to me what he lives on," she confessed. "He does no work down here and I've yet to hear what it is that he does in London."

"And yet he never has any money?" Anna mused.

"He's lazy, like his sister," Ellen said with disapproval. "I've always said so!"

Anna turned away. She wished she could make up her mind what to do. If she could see Michael, perhaps she could appeal to him to stay away from London. She had no faith that he would, but there was nothing else that she could do. She would warn Piran, but he would never believe that it wasn't she who had told Michael that they were in London. She sniffed to stop herself from crying.

"Did Piran leave an address?" she asked Ellen.

"Only the hospital," Ellen answered. "He didn't know

138

where he'd be staying."

Anna wrote a few words on a piece of paper. "Could you send him a telegram?" she murmured.

Ellen took the piece of paper, clutching it as though she would never let it go.

"I'll do it!" she said. She looked more like a gypsy than ever, eyeing Anna through half-shut, almost blind eyes. "If you want to find Mr. Michael, he's gone to St. Ives. They say he's looking for a place for someone to live over there. Some people said you might be thinking of it?" she added.

Anna stiffened. "Never!" she exploded. "Nothing short of dynamite is going to get me out of Chyanbara!"

Ellen trembled with silent laughter. "I don't think dynamite is what Mr. Piran will need," she said slyly.

Anna refused to answer. Was it so obvious? she wondered savagely. Did the whole world know she had fallen in love with Piran? Perhaps they had known before she had herself? But for the moment she didn't care.

Anna didn't stop to consider how she was going to find Michael Vaynor in the crowded streets of St. Ives. It didn't occur to her that she wouldn't find him. She got out the car, wishing that she wasn't so conscious of the empty space beside her where Peter's chair went. It was not the moment, she told herself fiercely, to lapse into sentimentality. But Wendy had upset her more than she knew and the mere thought of her made her feel sick. Whatever happened, she couldn't allow that evil, slithering female to ruin Piran's and Peter's lives any more than she already had.

She drove through Penzance in a blind fury, taking the road for St. Ives more by instinct than because she was concentrating on the route. The road was one that normally delighted her, passing through the remains of the earliest history of Cornwall. The small, square fields were unchanged from the times of the earliest tinners. Marked by banks of stones, the enormous boulders that lay at their foundation had been there since long before the Romans had come and defeated the Celtic rulers of the time. There were, too, vast empty spaces where no one seemed to live, and these she loved too. There was a hill, grey with outcrops of stone, where some film-maker had released a flock of goats who lived there to this day. Only a little further on was the ancient village of Zennor, where the legend was born of the mermaid who married a man and who lost him when he returned to his home. At Zennor, there was a stack of one of the most famous of the old tin mines too, and a small wayside museum where all things Cornish had been lovingly collected.

Anna passed it all by as if in a dream. Almost before she knew it, she was entering St. Ives, passing the glasshouses where a craftsman laid out his ivory for the sun to bleach it, and cruising down the hill towards the famous harbour where sooner or later everyone was wont to gather, the local inhabitants and the tourists alike.

She had some difficulty in finding somewhere to park the car, but at last she managed it, in a car park that stood high above the harbour with a superb view of the surrounding coast. In such a spot the old *huers* had looked for the shoals of pilchards for which Cornwall had once been so famous, for St. Ives had been one of the leading pilchard ports of Victorian times and earlier, until the fish had suddenly and mysteriously vanished from the Cornish seas.

Adjacent to the car park was another park for coaches, the nearest that they were allowed to go to the narrow streets in the hollow round the harbour. From there, passengers were taken up and down the hill by a series of smaller buses which ran a shuttlecock service back and forth. Anna boarded one of these and was hurtled down the hill, to be set down beside the harbour. It was only then that she wondered what she was going to do next. The street was crowded with people pushing their way back and forth, all of them busily engaged in getting somewhere. Only she seemed to have no idea where she wanted to go.

She glanced at her watch and saw that it was tea-time. Perhaps, she thought, she would have a cup of tea and then she would look for Michael. But she was beginning to realise the hopelessness of her task. The tears that she had so far held at bay threatened at the back of her throat again. Whatever had made her come?

She wandered into the nearest café and sat down at an empty table. A waitress came over immediately and Anna ordered a cup of tea.

"One Cornish tea," the waitress confirmed.

Anna felt that she could never bring herself to eat anything again, but she hadn't got the strength to argue. She felt truly miserable and she could feel herself trembling. She must be suffering from shock, she told herself bleakly, not really believing it, but the trembling went on despite the hot, sultry sunshine and the press of people all about her.

When the tea came, however, it looked so attractive that she found she was hungry. She remembered, without surprise, that she hadn't eaten the Cornish pasty that Ellen had brought her. She split the scones in half, buttered them, and filled them lavishly with jam and cream. It was very good indeed, she decided, and felt rather better. Even the trembling had stopped and she felt warmed and comforted by the hot, strong tea that the waitress had brought for her.

In fact she was so intent on what she was doing that she didn't notice the man who came across to her table and who sat down opposite her.

"You look awful!" he told her, wagging a finger in her face. "Shall I take pity on you and drive you home?"

"No!" She started, shivered, and started again. "Michael! Michael, I want to talk to you."

He smiled with easy confidence. "I knew it!" he teased her. "Sooner or later you had to fall for my fatal charm!"

She held on to the edge of the table so tightly that her knuckles shone white. "Don't go to London," she said urgently.

"Of course not, if you don't want me to," he answered easily. "Drink up, my lovely! Uncle Michael will look after you!"

CHAPTER TEN

"FEELING better?" Michael turned his head to glance at Anna, who was seated in the seat behind him.

"Much, thank you," she responded.

Perhaps, she thought to herself, she had maligned Michael, judging him entirely by their first unfortunate meeting? He had been kind enough today. When they had come out of the café, patches of cold sea-mist were already wafting up and down the narrow streets. It was strange how quickly these mists could blow up and cover the peninsula, no matter how hot and humid the day. Anna had had a mental picture of the rocky coast, wrapped in mist and history; a cosy respite from the cruel sea, flinging its might against these same shores whenever an Atlantic gale came this way. Then the thunderous might of the leaping water would make the ground tremble, but the granite rocks did not give way, and the sea did not gain its way by drowning the whole land. The sun would come out, or the mist would wrap the land in silence, and the sea would rest, gaining strength for the next battle. This was how Cornwall lived.

Michael's driving was very like himself. He used the horn a lot and accelerated and braked alternatively with a complete lack of respect for the mechanism of the vehicle he was man-handling. He tore out of St. Ives, swerving through the crowded streets with a curse for every straying pedestrian and a blast of the horn for every stationary car ahead of him. Once out of St. Ives, he slowed to a dawdle, muttering that after all they were not in any particular hurry.

"What brought you to St. Ives?" he asked Anna. The mist

wrapped them in silence which was broken only by the engine. Now and again, the sun burst through to light up the countryside, but the mist came rolling down the hills to obliterate the golden rays, and there would be nothing but its silver, silent presence once again.

"I came to find you," Anna said.

"I'm flattered!" he grinned.

She leaned forward, touching him on the shoulder. "Michael, don't go to London! Leave them alone."

His bright blue eyes met hers for an instant. "I don't know what you're talking about," he said.

She sighed. "Don't you? Aren't you going to London tonight?"

"If I am, I don't see what business it is of yours!" He sounded so indignant that, at another time, she might have been persuaded that he was innocent of anything more than minding his own affairs.

"Do you mean to say you won't visit Peter?" she asked sarcastically.

"He's my nephew," Michael retorted.

"He's Piran's son!"

Michael allowed the car to come to a complete stop. "That's sheer sentimentality," he told her. "Look, my pretty darling, why don't you keep your nose out of things that don't concern you?"

Anna gripped the seat on either side of her. "Why don't you?" she suggested.

To her surprise, Michael laughed. "Anna, my lovely, shall we both mind our own business and let the world go hang?"

She wondered if he were serious. "H-how?" she stammered.

"I'll make a bargain with you," he offered. "We'll spend the rest of the day amusing ourselves — and you'll be nice to me — and then I won't go to London."

144

She had a nightmare vision of what she might be letting herself in for.

"All right," she said with difficulty.

He smiled at her, the jaunty smile that she disliked so much because on him it was so conceited. "Cheer up!" he bade her. "I shan't take advantage of you today!"

She was immeasurably relieved. "I didn't think you would," she claimed, quite untruthfully. "I don't flatter myself that I hold out much attraction for you."

"Don't you?" he laughed heartily. "You underrate yourself, my dear. But this clammy mist is scarcely conducive, don't you think?"

Anna peered anxiously at the sky. It seemed to her fickle imagination that the mist was clearing. She crossed her fingers to bring good luck and wished earnestly that it would not.

"Wh-what do you want to do?" Her voice broke ominously and she cleared her throat officiously as if that was the only thing the matter with her.

"I don't know. I thought we might take a look round the local scenery," he answered. "Are you interested in that sort of thing?"

Under normal circumstances she would have been pleased. She was intensely interested in the old Cornish crosses that marked the places where the first Irish priests had preached the gospel to the pagan Celts; the older, prehistoric monuments, with their strange legends, such as the Merry Maidens turned to stone because they had danced on a Sunday; and the old industrial remains, the engine houses and their graceful stacks that are so typical of any Cornish scene.

"Lanyon Quoit is on the way," she said tentatively.

Michael seemed amused. "It's bang on the main road," he agreed. "I don't suppose Piran would grudge us the petrol to see something a little more remote!"

Anna cleared her throat again. "C-couldn't we begin there?" she suggested.

Michael frowned. "If you like," he said shortly.

He drove on in silence, braking sharply as they came within sight of what was left of the old prehistoric burial mound. What was left now was the skeleton structure of boulders, three in number, with another large flat stone covering all three as a roof. Other boulders lay close by, half-buried in the ground as, once, they all were before the earth was eroded away.

"Do you want to get out and take a look?" Michael asked, his distaste for the site evident in his every word.

At that moment the sun broke through the swirling mist again. "Yes," Anna said positively. "Yes, I'll get out. Don't bother to come, if you don't want to."

But Michael got languidly out of the car and went with her to the edge of the field. A few contented cattle nestled under the prehistoric roof, staring at them with as much interest as they had for the monument.

"Can one get in to see it better?" Anna suggested.

"I really don't know," Michael replied. He looked nervously at the cows. "Are you sure you want to?"

"Why not?" Anna laughed in sheer relief. "They won't do you any harm!"

"I'm not going to give them the chance!" Michael retorted. "But I'll help you over the fence, if you like?"

It was a more difficult climb than she had expected. Anna hoped that the farmer, on whose land the Quoit was, had not suffered too much from previous visitors. But she was no vandal and so she was completely sanguine that she would do no damage. She put her foot into Michael's hands and jumped neatly down on to the field. It was very rough, cut up by the hooves of the cows as they rubbed themselves against the ancient rocks.

Anna was interested to find how big the monument was. She herself could walk beneath it, pushing the cows away from her as she went. Whoever the strangers had been who had built such a barrow, they had certainly known their stuff. How odd it was, she thought, that this people had travelled so far, leaving their burial mounds all over Europe, and yet nothing was really known about them. No one knew what their beliefs had been, nor very much about how they had lived their lives sometimes in the misty past.

When she was ready to go back to the car, she couldn't see Michael. She thought for a minute that he was hiding behind the car, but there was no sign of him. For some reason, she had a premonitory twinge of fear.

"Michael!" she shouted.

He waved to her from a little way down the road. "I'm coming," he said.

She needed all his help to get back over the fence. "Where did you go?" she asked him.

"There's a sign there, pointing out the way to the old Ding-Dong mine," he told her.

She was intrigued. "Ding-Dong?"

He smiled. He was going out of his way to be agreeable to her, she thought. She wished she knew if she could trust him. Perhaps he too had been beguiled and manoeuvred by Wendy? She wished she didn't worry so much and, even more, she wished she knew what he was thinking.

"It used to have a bell," he told her. "At least, I think I've got the story right. The bell was taken away and is stored in a church – Madron, I expect, as we're in Madron parish."

"Can one go and look at it?" Anna pleaded.

Michael nodded. "I don't think we can take the car. We'll have to walk."

He took the car down to the turning, though, backing it into the narrow track. "It'll be ready for when we leave," he said.

It was a strange way of enjoying themselves, Anna thought, as they walked briskly down the track towards the disused mine. Most of the time, she couldn't even see the stack, as it was lost in the mist that seemed to be getting thicker all the time.

"Do you really want to do this?" Anna asked him curiously.

"Why not?" he shrugged.

"I don't know," she admitted. "I hadn't seen you as the outdoor type."

"Certainly not!" Michael exclaimed with horror. "Indoor games are much more in my line!"

"Then why –?"

"I have my better moments," he told her. "Isn't this the sort of thing you want to do?"

"Well, yes," she admitted. She could think of better times to go sightseeing, she thought. She shivered slightly as a patch of mist caught them in its damp fingers. "Do you think this mist will last?"

Michael screwed up his face and studied the bright, white shape which was the sun. "It might clear in the late evening," he said.

He showed no sign of turning back, so Anna decided that he must be keener to see the old mine than he would admit. Cornwall's old mines and engine houses *were* of interest to most men. People from all over the world came to this south-westerly corner of England, even today, to learn their trade, and in past times Cornish engineers had left to work the mines of other nations all over the world. Anna wasn't quite so interested. It was true she wanted to see one of these old engine houses and its accompanying stack, but not on a day like this, with the damp cold penetrating her very bones.

"Let's run!" Michael said suddenly. "It'll be warmer." He pulled the scarf he was wearing in his open-necked shirt closer to him. "Come on!"

Anna did her best to follow him, but she was afraid to go too fast along a track that she didn't know and could hardly see. It was practically unused and great tufts of grass had grown amongst the beaten down earth that formed the path. There had been a time when the first part at least had had a tarmac surface, but this had long since disintegrated into a series of ruts, and finally petered out altogether.

Michael had got a long way ahead. Anna gave up trying to catch up with him and steadied into a quick walk. She had a stitch in her side and when she tried to take a deep breath the sea-mist caught in her throat and choked her.

The feeling that she had had of impending disaster increased when the chimney stack of the old mine suddenly loomed up before her and disappeared again.

"Michael!" she called out.

But there was no answer.

"Michael! Please!" she sobbed.

His hands grasped her and he laughed. "I believe you're scared!" he taunted her. He laughed again. "I'm not complaining! I like a girl to be a little scared!"

Anna shook herself, trying to still the rising panic within her. "It's only the mist," she said. "It's difficult to tell where one is. I saw the stack for a minute and then it disappeared again."

"It isn't much further," he confirmed.

Anna came to a stop. "Couldn't we go back?" she asked him.

"I believe you really are afraid!" he said impatiently. "We're much too close to go back now."

Anna shivered. "You can do as you like, *I'm* going back!" She felt his fingers on her arm, tightening their grip on her. "Let me go!"

"Have you forgotten our agreement so quickly?" he inquired softly.

"N-no. But I hardly think this is much fun for either of us," she answered with spirit.

"*I'm* having fun!" he assured her.

She looked down at her watch. There was still hours to go before the night train left for London. There was nothing for it, she would have to trail after him through the fog for as long as she could. If she parted company with him, he would go, she knew that, and then what chance would Piran and Peter have of ever coming to an understanding? Her eyes stung with tears and she couldn't find her handkerchief. They must have walked at least a mile from the road, she thought. Could the Ding-Dong mine have been so far away?

The next moment she very nearly walked into it.

"Stay on the path," Michael bade her. "I forgot to warn you of the dangers of falling into disused shafts around here. You might never be heard of again!" he added with a laugh.

Anna thought it was no laughing matter.

"Is that why you brought me?" she asked him sharply.

He was hurt. "My dear Anna, you really do dislike me, don't you?"

She shook her head. "No. No, I don't. You've been very kind," she said.

"Then what are you so worried about?" he asked reasonably.

"I don't know," she admitted. "You see, Wendy came to see me –"

"I gathered that much!" he said sharply. "What did she say?"

"That's just it," Anna sighed. She hesitated, but then she couldn't believe that he would have had anything to do with his own sister's unhappiness. "I think she drove Caroline away," she burst out.

Michael turned and faced her. In the still thickening mist, his face looked as grey as the surrounding scenery. "What do you mean?" he said.

"I know it sounds impossible," Anna appealed to him. "I thought so at first. But Wendy was engaged to Piran before he ever set eyes on your sister. Even when he married her, I don't think she accepted that she'd lost him at all. She began to plan as to how she could get rid of Caroline almost at once. And that's not all," she added unhappily. "She's hoping to get rid of Peter on you, and for me to go away, and then she'll have Piran all to herself again!"

Michael smiled his particularly irritating, arrogant yet jaunty smile. "I don't believe a word of it!" he said.

"But you must!" Anna insisted.

"Why? So that you can marry Piran instead?" She could tell how much the idea of her being in love with Piran riled him. The blood ebbed away from her cheeks as the conviction grew that Michael really was attracted to her.

"I don't think he wants to marry anyone," she said slowly.

"That doesn't mean that you're not in love with him!" he retorted.

"Perhaps not." She was too honest to deny it. "But it was a wicked thing to do!"

"If you ask me," he said, his interest fast evaporating, "it's a wicked thing to say about Wendy. I've seen her trying to be-friend Peter, but the little devil won't have anything to do with her. In fact the only person he has any time for at all is me. It's been the same ever since Piran turned his back on him in the hospital in London!"

"You mean Peter *thought* he had – with your help!" Anna put in bitterly.

"It's a two-way affection," Michael said. "I'm fond enough of the boy, come to that!"

"How fond?" Anna demanded.

"Enough to wish to give him a happier life than he's had hidden away down here –"

"At his own expense!" Anna interrupted him, outraged.

Michael shrugged. "Why not? I haven't a penny."

"Then what do you live on?" Anna retorted.

Michael gave her a restrained smile. "Drop the subject, Anna, my dear. I won't quarrel with you, no matter how much you provoke me. I'd far rather take you inside the engine house and kiss your suspicions out of you!"

Anna's eyes opened wide. "You said you wouldn't!" she claimed.

"And I'm a man of my word. My only intention is to show you over the place – that is, if we can get inside. You'll find it very interesting if we can."

Anna was silent. She wished she had never come with him. The mist was thicker than ever and she was afraid of the old, crumbling building and what they might find within. Reason told her that it couldn't be anything very dreadful, but supposing, just supposing that a family of rats, or some other vermin, had made it their home? She was frankly relieved to see that someone had blocked their way with barbed wire.

"Perhaps it's dangerous," she suggested.

"Nonsense! It's safe enough as long as you look where you're going. Look, we can climb in there."

He gave Anna a little push towards the opening. Her muscles felt stiff and awkward, but he insisted, so she obediently climbed through the wire and pushed her way into the derelict building.

It was a moment or two before her eyes grew accustomed to the gloomy interior. The machinery which had once dominated the mine had been taken away, but she thought she could see, even now, how it had worked. Apart from having a good lode and the captains skilled enough to get the stuff out of the earth, the important thing was to have an adequate pump. The winters in Cornwall are often wet and there had been several quite rich mines which had had to be abandoned because of water troubles. Hence the necessity for drainage, which in turn had led to these magnificent buildings that covered West Cornwall from one end to the other.

"It's a shame there's not many of these old places in action," Michael commented as he crawled in beside her. "Cornish pumping machines are the best in the world. Did you know that when the Dutch want to reclaim land from the sea they use Cornish machines?"

Anna hadn't known. She could imagine, though, where the steam cylinder had gone, coupled as it must have been to one end of a vast rocking beam overhead. The other end of the beam, she supposed, would have operated the plunger pumps in the shaft of the mine.

"It must have been a colossal bit of machinery," she said.

Michael made a disparaging gesture. "Hardly one of the biggest! Still, I expect it raised a fair quantity of water at every stroke of the piston in the cylinder."

"How fast do you suppose it went?" Anna asked.

"That's the sort of thing Piran knows the answer to," he said. "I believe it was about eight strokes to the minute, but I can't make the same convincing answers that he delights in. Who wants to know anyway?"

"I do," she said.

"You make a good pair!" he snorted.

He prowled about for a few minutes longer, testing the

brickwork with his fingers. "They made these places to last!" he said at last with grudging approval. "I'm going to take a look at the outside."

"No! Please don't!" Anna cried out. "One can hardly see at all now!"

He grinned at her. "I shan't be long," he said pacifically. "You can wait for me here. You can hardly get lost in here!"

She watched him go with a sinking heart. The shadows in the corners of the building oppressed her. Here and there she could see where a spider had spun its fine web, catching the dust from the disintegrating brickwork. It was only her imagination, of course, but she thought she could hear the old bell tolling in the gloomy heights above her, and she was afraid.

She waited for a long time. At first she thought she could hear his footsteps on the outside of the building and the noise comforted her. But then, for a long time, there was only silence. She couldn't wait any longer, she decided. Not by herself in that gloomy half-darkness, listening to the silence all about her.

She tried to push her way out the way she had come, but it wasn't as easy as she had remembered. Some loose bricks, barbed wire, and some heavy pieces of wood barred her way. She pushed against them as hard as she could, but they refused to give. She was in a complete panic now. She forced herself to take a number of even, deep breaths to steady herself. If she removed the bricks one at a time, she would soon be out, she told herself. It was very, very important to get out of that confined space into the open! Even the mist was preferable to the silent decay of the engine house!

It took her a long time to push the bricks out one by one. They were few in number, but they had been firmly wedged into position by the rotting planks that she was quite sure had not been there before.

"Michael!" she shouted. "Michael, Michael!" But the sound of her voice came back to her from the mist as from a solid wall. Of Michael there was no sign at all.

At last she scrambled out of the opening and, almost on her hands and knees, searched for the neglected track that led back to the main road. It was hard to be certain where it began. Everything looked strange in the ghostly grey of the enclosing mist.

When she found the track, she stumbled along it, terrified that she would lose her way and fall down one of the disused shafts that pocketed the surrounding hills. She no longer called Michael. It had been a deliberate attempt to shut her inside the engine house, she was almost certain, and she was almost more afraid of meeting him than of being alone.

If it had seemed long going in the other direction, this time she thought that she would never get to the road. The sea-mist, that earlier in the afternoon had seemed playful and of no importance, was now so thick that she could only see a few feet in any direction. It distorted the sound of her own foot-steps and breathing and she had to fight the panic that threatened to engulf her if she would let it. But she wouldn't! She might weep a little, and shiver from the cold, but she would not give in! She would find the road if it was the last thing she did.

She was close to despair, however, when she had spent half an hour walking away from the Ding-Dong mine. Once she had thought she had heard a car behind her, and yet she knew that she hadn't crossed the road. Then, when she least ex-pected it, she put out a hand and touched a post. The feel of the wood made her jump until she had made quite sure what it was. With a sigh of relief, she could just make out the letters: Ding-Dong. She had reached the road.

How long she stood there, wet and shivering, she never knew. It was a long time, she knew that much. It was almost as if she were afraid to move. Instead, she searched the trails of mist with strained eyes, hoping to catch a glimpse of the car. But even as she did so, she knew it had gone.

When she had summoned up sufficient courage, she walked a short way back up the path and then along the road to make sure that Michael hadn't merely moved it, but there was nothing there. She should have known, she thought dully. The words that Wendy had uttered came back to mock her: "He won't listen to you. He's already sold out to me!" Anna couldn't think why she hadn't guessed it before, why Michael never seeemed to work, and why Wendy had been so sure of him. She had *paid* him to take Peter off her hands. And paid him handsomely at that!

When Anna came back to the turning to the Ding-Dong mine, she could see the tracks of the car where it had been parked. On the edge of the road alongside she found one of Peter's rugs that Michael had shoved out of the car, and pinned to it was a note. She was aware of an overwhelming sense of relief that he had not intended her to be immured in the engine house for ever, though it might have come to much the same thing had she become as hysterical as she had felt.

She unfolded the note with numb fingers. Her clothes, everything, felt damp and cold to her touch.

Keep warm, the note said. *I'm sorry, my dear, truly sorry. But I know which side my bread is buttered. Do you? Michael.*

Clutching the rug about her, Anna had made her way back to the mine. It was shelter of a sort and she was of no mind to die of exposure during the night. For a minute she had entertained the idea that some car would come along and rescue her, but nobody in their right mind would be going anywhere

156

until the mist cleared. She had staggered along the path, intent on finding somewhere dry to spend the night, and she had succeeded in that. She had wrapped the rug right round herself and curled herself up into a tight ball in a corner of the disused building. And she had cried herself to sleep.

The light from the torch hurt her eyes as she struggled into consciousness. She gulped and cowered back in fear when she saw the tall, dark shape of a man standing beside her. Then she saw it was Piran.

"I got your telegram," he told her.

She rubbed her eyes, knowing that she looked a mess and wishing that he would turn the torch away from her.

"How did you know I was here?" she asked him.

Piran looked decidedly grim. "I went to the station at Penzance in time for the train. I choked it out of him before sending him on his way."

"Oh." She was silent for a minute. "I did try," she said.

He smiled at her. She was quite extraordinarily aware of him and she knew that she was blushing. "So I see, my love. So I see." And he gathered her into his arms and allowed her to cry her fright out into his shoulder in peace.

Outside, the mist had completely disappeared.

CHAPTER ELEVEN

"HUSH, darling, if you cry any more you'll feel awful in the morning!"

"I feel awful now!" she assured him, her voice muffled by the warm material of his coat.

"I'm sure you do. But you have to stop some time!" His exasperated sympathy made her want to laugh, and then she was crying again, the tears pouring down her face.

"I'm so sorry!" she said. "Don't pay any attention. I *can't* stop!"

His arms tightened about her. "Whoever would have thought it of the cool, calm and collected Miss Anna St. James!"

Anna sobbed. "You never bothered to get to know her!" she complained.

He soothed her as best he could. "Darling, I know you were badly frightened, but this won't do!"

She sniffed. "Anyone would think that I wasn't *trying* to stop!" she muttered, feeling decidedly sorry for herself.

"Heaven forbid that I should ever see you when you *weren't* trying!" Piran retorted bracingly. "Anna, this has got to stop!"

"But I can't!"

She wouldn't have blamed him if he had slapped her. It would, she thought, have been a fitting ending to the day. She struggled to free herself from his warmth and the hardness of his chest in an earnest effort to pull herself together. Her eyes, two dark, moist pools of agony, met his.

"Oh, Piran," she whispered, "I'm so cold! I don't think I'll ever be warm again."

She had stopped crying now quite suddenly, and was shivering instead. She tried to stop her teeth chattering because the sound of it distressed her.

"I'll take you home," he said.

She nodded briefly and struggled to her feet, unwrapping the rug from her cramped limbs. It would be the best thing to do, she thought. For now that she had stopped crying, she couldn't bear him to be kind to her. Kindness was the last emotion she wanted to inspire and she would have given anything at that moment to have been swept into his arms and kissed until she was warm again. But that wasn't Piran's way. He would only do that to a girl he really loved and he didn't love her at all!

Piran went out first, helping her as she followed him. Even her hands felt bruised and sore, as she clung to his in an effort to stay upright and to force herself to walk along the track to the road again.

There was not a sign of the mist that had entrapped her earlier. The stars shone big in the moonlit sky, for, at this time of year, even at eleven o'clock at night, it never seems really dark. Anna sniffed the air, expecting to be able to smell the salt-sea smell of the mist, but even that had gone. The night was as smooth and languorous as a night in the tropics, with the air as smooth as silk.

What had seemed so endless before proved to be quite a short way back to the road. Anna judged that she had been right the first time she had walked along it, and that it was about a mile. In Piran's company, she wouldn't have greatly cared if they had gone on walking all night.

"I still don't understand," she said, "how you knew where to find me."

"I took the first train back from London when I got your wire," he told her. There was something in his voice that made

159

her feel almost sorry for Michael Vaynor – sorry for Wendy too!

"And what about Peter?" She wished she didn't sound so anxious, in case he should think that she didn't believe that Peter would soon be walking again.

Piran gave her an odd look. "Ah yes, Peter," he said. "He's enjoying himself, I think –"

"But what did they say?" she insisted.

"The boy made me promise not to tell you," he answered apologetically. "What I am to tell you about is that the Trethowyns have decided to get together and be a real family in the future. I think Michael is going to be disappointed by his reception in London!"

"Oh, Piran! Really? Are you sure?" she pressed him.

"We had time to talk," he said simply.

They had reached the car before she had time to ask him anything else. The questions crowded into her mind, but she was too exhausted to make much sense of them, and it seemed he understood, for he smiled very gently at her and said, "It will keep. I'll tell you all about it in the morning."

It was the same car that she had driven to St. Ives and that Michael had offered to drive her back to Penzance in; it was the same car that he had driven off, leaving her alone with only the Ding-Dong mine and the mist for company. Anna could not forbear a shiver as Piran opened the door for her and helped her in, wrapping her round with warming rugs.

"We'll soon be home," he told her. His smile was so gentle that she was afraid that she would cry again.

"I'm quite all right now," she said. "There's no need to worry about me, you know."

"None at all!" he teased her. But it was the same impersonal teasing that she had come to know so well.

"Piran, you are sure that Peter won't change his mind when

160

he sees Michael?"

"I'm certain," he answered. "The boy is no fool and he told me some of the things you had said to him. Anna, I'm grateful. Somehow or other you've achieved what I quite failed to do, and returned my son to me."

Anna was embarrassed. "I *like* Peter," she said.

She wondered why he laughed, but it wasn't easy to talk once he had climbed into the driving seat and started up the engine. She was too tired to lean forward to catch his words and she couldn't think straight about what she was saying herself.

It seemed hardly any time before they drew up outside Piran's house. He drove straight into the garage and switched off the engine.

"I've told Ellen to prepare a bedroom for you in the house," he said, as he helped her out of the car.

"I'd rather go home –" she began.

He put his arm around her and half-carried her towards the back door. "No arguments! Besides," he added gruffly, "you *are* home!"

The light from the kitchen made her blink, but Ellen was kind.

"Come on now, Miss Anna. I'll run a bath for you while you're getting out of those clothes. I'll bring your food to you in bed."

"I don't think I want anything," Anna protested.

Ellen shook her head at her. "You'll do just as I tell you, my handsome. Hurry along now, or you'll be asleep before you're ready."

It was nice to be loved and scolded, Anna thought as she stumbled up the stairs. It was nice to be at home.

When she awoke, she could see St. Michael's Mount silhouetted in the morning light and standing in a sea of gold. For a moment she wondered where she was and by the time she had remembered she was asleep again.

"Miss Anna! Miss Anna!"

Anna stirred and grunted. "Yes?" she murmured.

"Miss Anna! I've brought your breakfast!"

Anna stirred over and saw Ellen towering over her bed with a tray in her hands. "Breakfast?"

Ellen put the tray down on a table and came back to the bed. "Up with you!" she commanded. She plumped up the pillows to her own satisfaction and then allowed Anna to lean back against them.

"I hardly ever eat breakfast," Anna said sleepily.

"You'll eat it today!" Ellen said with certainty. "We all eat breakfast in this household like Christians, and you'll do the same."

Anna meekly accepted the tray. The scrambled eggs, sausage and bacon smelt simply delicious.

"Oh, Ellen! You're spoiling me!" she accused her.

Ellen was pleased. "Time somebody did! You'll find some coffee in that pot and the toast is wrapped in your napkin." She went to the window and looked out, before adjusting the windows to let in a little more air. "You get a fine view from these windows," she remarked.

Anna nodded eagerly. "I saw St. Michael's Mount at dawn," she said.

"I wouldn't have thought you'd have been awake," Ellen laughed. "Sleeping like a baby you were when I came in."

Anna grinned. "The sleep of the just!" she chuckled.

Ellen gave her a sharp look. "Maybe. There's some that should have got mighty little last night, if that's the case!"

Anna blushed faintly. "Never mind, it all came right in the end," she said brightly.

"We'll hope so!" Ellen agreed darkly. "We'll hope so. But there's no knowing what *some* people will do!" She tossed her head to make her point the better and went to the door. "Come down when you're ready. Mr. Piran has already gone out, but you'll find me in the kitchen."

Anna made no effort to hurry to get up. She ate her breakfast leisurely, savouring every mouthful. Then she read the newspapers that Ellen had put on the side of her tray from cover to cover. Only then did she swing her legs over the side of the bed and take a look at the clothes that Ellen had fetched for her from Chyanbara. It was not perhaps the choice she would have made for herself, but she climbed into them and went downstairs to find Ellen.

"Ah, there you are!" the Cornish woman greeted her. "Come in, dearie, and make yourself comfortable."

Anna hesitated. "I thought I'd go back to the cottage," she said. "I haven't any make-up here and there are things I want to do."

"No!" Ellen snapped. "No," she went on in a calmer voice, "Mr. Piran said you were not to set foot outside the house until he gets back. If there's anything you're wanting, I'll fetch it for you."

"But I want to go," Anna explained carefully. "You've been very good to me, Ellen, but I have my work to do."

"That? It'll keep."

"That's what you think!" Anna answered with a laugh. "Why don't you come over yourself later?"

Ellen dried her hands on the apron she was wearing. "If you've set your mind on going, I'll come with you," she said, her voice tight with disapproval.

Anna blinked. "But it isn't far, or anything," she objected.

"You're not going down there on your own and that's the end of it!" Ellen sniffed. "I'd never hear the end of it – not

163

from Mr. Piran, nor from the boy either!"

Anna's eyes lit up. "Have you heard about Peter?"

Ellen nodded. "He'll be back in a couple of days – on his feet most likely! And we know who we have to thank for that!"

"The surgeon? I don't know. I think the physiotherapist has done him a lot of good, don't you?"

Ellen's eyes filled with tears. It was unlike her, Anna thought, to be so sentimental, but then she was probably very fond of Peter, especially as she had had more to do with his upbringing in the last three years than anyone else. "And did you have nothing to do with it?" the Cornish woman asked her tartly.

Anna blushed. "Not really," she denied quickly. "Peter did most of it himself."

"Well, I wouldn't have believed it!" Ellen said stoutly. "Nothing would make him do his exercises before, just as nothing would make him say a civil word to Mr. Piran. But Mr. Piran says that's all over now. And who else has he got to thank but you for that, I'd like to know?"

Anna smiled faintly. "I think some people deliberately tried to mislead Peter about his father," she said mildly.

"That's as may be!" Ellen answered flatly. "There are some who'll be moving away from here, and then maybe we'll have a bit of peace!"

"Maybe," Anna teased her.

Ellen clucked her tongue in sudden agitation. "Now where is Mr. Piran? He said he'd be back before you would want to go over to Chyanbara."

"But, Ellen," Anna said gently, "I really don't need anyone to hold my hand –"

"You haven't seen it!"

Anna gave Ellen a look of shock, her freckles more obvious

164

than usual against her white skin. "Well, I'm going to see it now!"

She wrenched open the back door and started across the lawn, not caring whether Ellen was following her or not. It was a truly beautiful day, hot from the sun, but with a lift from the cooling breeze that had not been in the air for days. It was difficult to believe that only the day before the mist had come swirling in from the sea, for now it was so clear that Anna could see the faint line of the Lizard behind St. Michael's Mount and right beyond Mousehole on the other side.

Ellen came running behind her. "Shall I go in first?" she panted.

Anna shook her head. "It's my house," she said. She unlocked the door and pushed it open, ducking her head to get inside. It looked exactly as she had left it and she breathed a sigh of relief, for her nerves were ragged after the night before.

"There you are!" she said. "There's nothing to make such a fuss about!"

"No," said Ellen uncertainly.

Anna sat down on the settle and studied the wide old hearth with friendly eyes. In the winter, she thought, if she was still there, she would burn only sweet-smelling wood and pinecones.

In some agitation, Ellen picked up the corner of one of the dust-sheets Anna had spread over her work the day before. "It's here," she said in an expressionless voice. "Mr. Piran saw them last night and he covered them up. He didn't want you to find them by yourself."

"Find what?" Anna stood up slowly and went over to the table. The little serpentine bottles that she had so carefully made had been ground into dust. Someone had beaten them with a hammer, so hard that there was nothing left of them ex-

165

cept a multi-coloured sand.

"But who —? What —?" Anna stammered. "How she must hate me," she said in strained tones.

"Mr. Piran has gone to see her," Ellen told her. "I've never seen a man so angry as he was last night when he came here!"

"He came here?" Anna frowned. "I thought he came straight from the station to the Ding-Dong mine?"

Ellen shook her head slowly. "He saw Mr. Michael on to the train," she explained. "He waited for that. But then he came here. He told me to make up a bed in the house for you and he called in here to get you a coat. But he never did more than see these."

"I wish he hadn't," said Anna.

"Ay, it was a shock for the poor man. But he had to know some time."

Anna looked sad. "No. If I'd seen them first, I'd have put them in the dustbin," she said firmly. "It's where that sort of thing belongs!"

"I hadn't thought she had the strength in her," Ellen remarked.

"Nor would I," Anna agreed. She swallowed hard. "Oh well, there's no use in standing around like this, is there? Let's sweep it all away and forget all about it. I can easily make some more — not that I expect Wendy will ever use them at the Meadhouse."

"Perhaps she won't have any say in the matter," Ellen said piously.

Anna thought that was wishful thinking, but she said nothing. She got a dustpan and brush out and began to sweep up the mess on the table. It was a solid, wooden affair that she had bought for its toughness and its suitability as a workbench. She noted without much emotion that pieces of serpentine were embedded deep in the wood. She would never be

166

able to get them out and those that she could left deep holes in the surface that would be difficult to fill.

"Here's Mr. Piran now," Ellen said suddenly, with such obvious relief that Anna smiled. "I'll tell him where you are!" She ran out of the door, waving her arms in the air to attract his attention. Anna could hear him saying that he thought he had asked her not to allow Anna to go to the cottage.

"She'd made up her mind," Ellen said stubbornly.

Piran laughed. "I can imagine!" he exclaimed sharply. "Never mind, Ellen, go back to the house. I'll talk to her."

Anna could feel her muscles tensing as he approached the house. It was ridiculous to be so affected by any man! She went on sweeping, with the same, monotonous movements. He was going to be *kind* again, she thought, and she didn't see how she was going to bear it.

"Hullo," she said dully as he bent to come in at the door.

"Hullo, yourself!"

He sounded unbearably cheerful. Anna looked at his suspiciously. "What did I ever do to her to make her hate me so much?" she asked.

"I don't know. It was rather horrible." At least he wasn't going to pretend that he didn't understand how she felt about it.

"They were only little bottles!" Anna murmured, her voice raw with emotion.

Piran put his hands on her shoulders and turned her round to face him. "Thank God she didn't get her hands on you!" was all he said. "She came to see you here yesterday, didn't she?"

"Yes," said Anna.

He took the dustpan and brush out of her hands and put them on the table, covering the whole lot with the dust sheet.

"Let's sit down," he suggested.

She sat down on the settle, feeling defeated. How could anyone deliberately beat into a pulp something, no matter how they felt about its creator? It made her feel slightly sick to think of the sheer, violent hatred that had inspired such destruction.

"She told me she wanted to buy the bottles after all," she said dully.

"Did she?" he encouraged her gently.

Anna took a deep breath. "Piran," she began, "I don't want to interfere in your affairs, certainly not something which was finished so long ago –"

"Something to do with Wendy?" he asked her, his eyes half-closed.

She nodded painfully. "You were engaged to her once, weren't you? At least that's what she said." She hesitated and then went on wearily, "Wendy never forgave or forgot."

"So I gather," Piran said dryly. "I've just come from the Meadhouse. Wendy is selling out her share of the business. She's going to live with her father in London."

Anna was startled into a smile. "Oh well, perhaps the rest doesn't matter, then," she said.

"I think it does," Piran contradicted her. "We've had too many secrets in the past. If we'd talked things out before, perhaps some of these things need never have happened."

"Even if it concerns Caroline?" she asked him.

"Perhaps especially if it concerns Caroline," he said.

She twisted her fingers nervously together. "Wendy tried to make me go away," she said suddenly.

"Did you say you would?" he asked.

Anna shook her head. "I don't like being blackmailed," she said proudly. "Besides, I kept telling her that it wasn't such a big thing for me to sell some serpentine bottles to her. I had to fulfil my other contracts first. When she saw she couldn't

168

move me, she began to tell me about Caroline. Somehow or other. She told me, she had managed to persuade Caroline that you didn't love her any more –"

"But Caroline knew better than that!" Piran exclaimed.

"She didn't!" Anna exclaimed.

"She must have done! Why did she suppose I married her?"

Anna couldn't resist giving him a mocking look. "A mental aberration, I expect," she suggested.

Piran was outraged. "You didn't know Caroline! She was one of the loveliest creatures I've ever seen!"

"And yet Wendy managed to persuade her that she was an overblown rose, likely to go to seed at any moment," Anna told him dryly.

"What?" His scandalised cry hurt her. That he was badly hurt himself, she had no difficulty in believing. "I don't believe it! Caroline was – well, she wasn't very sensible. She was very like Michael to look at, only gentler and more perfect in every way. How could she have believed that?"

"I imagine Wendy was quite persuasive," Anna said dryly.

"Go on," Piran said after a minute. "I'd better hear it all."

"It isn't an easy thing to say," Anna went on. "You see, Wendy thought she was in love with you. Perhaps she is, in her own way. Poor Caroline got in her way."

Piran had a defeated look that made Anna wince. She wished she could have spared him ever having to know about his wife, but in justice to her he had to know.

"I thought Wendy and Caroline were friends," he said forlornly.

"I think Wendy meant you to think that. She waited for a long, long time to get her own way. What I can't understand is why, when she'd succeeded in driving Caroline away, she didn't marry you herself at once. She didn't like Peter being here, of course, but she was far more likely to get rid of him once she was your wife."

Piran smiled sourly. "I never asked her!"

"*That* wouldn't stop her!" Anna retorted.

"That's what you think, Miss St. James! Even in this age of female independence, a man can't be married out of hand without having some say in the matter!"

Anna laughed. "Do you know what I think?" she said confidentially. "I think Wendy was paying Michael to tempt Peter away from you. Once he had Peter in his care, he could use the boy's own money, but before that he had to live on something, didn't he?"

Piran sighed. "I daresay you're right."

"But you're sure that's all right now?" she insisted gravely.

"Absolutely. Peter is buying Wendy out of the firm. In future it will be entirely a Trethowyn enterprise. What do you think of that?'

Anna's expression softened. "I'm very glad for you," she said. "When will Peter be back?"

"In a day or so. They're fitting him up with crutches until his legs get a bit stronger. In another year he can go away to school."

"Away?" Anna put her hand over her mouth. It wouldn't matter to her, she reminded herself. Peter might even want to go away to school.

"You don't approve?" Piran asked with an amused smile. "But he needs to go to school. He needs friends of his own age. But he'll be around quite a lot too. You'll be able to see him as often as you want – more often!" he added with a grin.

"Perhaps I shan't be here," Anna defended herself.

"I think you will be," Piran said with calm certainty.

"How can you know that?" she demanded. "I'm not sure that I *like* living in Cornwall –"

"But —" he began.

"It hasn't been at all *comfortable*," she murmured. "I like Chyanbara, but I can't forget the way Wendy smashed up those bottles! I can feel her hatred for me all round."

"You don't have to live here," he protested.

"I can't change now," she answered. "The season will be beginning in earnest soon. I wouldn't be able to get in anywhere."

He smiled. The light had come back into his eyes and some of the arrogance had come back into his face. "As to that," he said, "I have some ideas about that! I promise you one thing, Wendy need never worry you ever again, I'll see to that. Can't you wait a few days?" he pleaded.

"How long?" she asked him.

"Until Peter gets back?"

Her brow cleared. "Oh yes! I'll wait until then." She chuckled. "He's my landlord, after all! He might even expect a month's notice from me."

"Peter will do as he's told!" Piran said fiercely. "None of my family will ever worry you again!"

So that was it, Anna thought. It was all over. He was telling her as nicely as possible that he didn't care what she did! She could stay, or she could go, it made no difference to him.

"I'll stay until Peter gets back," she repeated, fighting the tears in the back of her throat.

Piran gave her a smile of complete satisfaction. "Good," he said. "In justice to Caroline, I have to give her a few days to mourn her as I should have mourned her when she died. You do see that, don't you?"

She nodded, not seeing at all.

"She's such an insubstantial ghost," he went on. "A friendly ghost, for she would have loved you for finding out the truth.

171

But not even her ghost can be allowed to come between us in the future, so I must have a few days to give to her –"

Anna didn't understand a word he was saying to her.

"I think I'd better help Ellen with the lunch," she said.

CHAPTER TWELVE

THE week slipped by quite quickly – Anna was surprised to discover just how quickly. It was true that she managed to do a great deal of work, but she had thought that she would have found it an intolerably lonely time, and it hadn't been. Indeed, she had been emotionally numbed and was glad of the respite, to be herself and to be by herself. Of Piran she saw nothing at all. Ellen told her that he had gone up to London to visit Peter, but she knew when he came back because there was a sudden blaze of activity at the Trethowyn house as it was cleaned from top to bottom. She was mildly hurt that he didn't even visit her, but she refused to allow herself to think about it. By the time Peter came home, it would be necessary for her to have all her defences in order. There was, however, no sign of his coming.

Then, late in the evening, when Anna was just putting the final touches to a batch of jewellery she was sending to London before going to bed, Piran knocked at her door.

"May I come in?" he asked.

She nodded, defiantly aware that her defences were crumbling at the first whiff of the battle to come. She went on packing up the parcel, ticking the items off against her list.

Piran stood in the doorway, smiling.

"I came to tell you that Peter comes home tomorrow," he said. "Would you like to come to the station to meet him?"

Although it was only eight o'clock in the morning the sun was already quite hot. From the platform, Anna could see its rays dancing on the sea. It would not be long now before Peter's train came in.

"Are you sure he won't need his chair?" she asked Piran nervously.

Piran gave her an infectious grin. "Still worrying?" he teased her.

"I'm trying not to," she assured him.

His laughter was affectionate. "Anna, my love, I believe you're looking forward to seeing Peter more than I am!"

"You saw him when you went to London!" she returned. "I haven't seen him since he went away."

He looked at her with amused eyes. "No more you have," he said gently.

It was Piran who saw the approaching train first. It came hurtling past the heliport and down the track into the station, with the curiously blind look that night sleepers have. The dust on the platform lifted in the wind and fell again on to their shoes and round the legs of the platform seats. A couple of porters walked slowly down the platform to the first class berths, chatting to each other as they went.

Anna hopped up and down, hoping to see Peter immediately, but although doors were flung open up and down the train there was no sign of him. A few dishevelled passengers stepped out and looked anxiously about them. Some of them had obviously come on holiday, but here and there was someone who lived locally and who knew exactly where they were going. The second wave of passengers took longer leaving the train and were as smart as if they had just stepped out of their own houses. The porters loaded their baggage on to trailers and pushed the mounds of suitcases and baskets towards the main entrance of the station.

"He isn't on it!" Anna exclaimed.

"He won't hurry off," Piran answered her. "He hates asking for help when there's a crowd all round him."

"But he will ask?" Anna asked impatiently.

"He'll ask the attendant, unless he sees me first," Piran assured her. "He's used to it by this time."

But she wondered if any boy could ever be "used to it"? It made it all the more wonderful to think that soon he would be walking, running, just like any other boy of his age.

"There he is!" she exclaimed suddenly.

"Where?"

Anna pointed to the window where she had caught a glimpse of Peter's black hair. "I was beginning to think he hadn't come!" she said in relief.

They hurried down the platform towards the window and joined the huddle of people round the open door who were sorting out their luggage and where they were going in loud accents, so at variance with the softer sounds of the speech of the local people.

"Why don't you go on and get him?" Anna prodded Piran, but he shook his head.

"He'll come out when he's ready."

The crowd moved away, following their luggage as it moved away in the capable hands of one of the porters. Now, Anna thought, now surely he must come! She kept her eyes fixed on the doorway and was finally rewarded by catching a glimpse of him standing by the side of the attendant. He waved to her and grinned and she waved back, so nervous that she could hardly speak. He was so tall!

He leaned out of the door and placed his crutches firmly on the platform, before putting first one foot and then the other down between them. He was quite as tall as Piran! Indeed, they looked incredibly alike, with their dark good looks and the arrogant set of their shoulders.

"Oh, Peter!" Anna breathed.

He was naïvely pleased. "Surprised?" he teased her.

She nodded, unable to speak. He manipulated himself slowly towards her, grinning at her. He was so *big* to be only thirteen! What a difference it made, when you had never seen anyone except when they were sitting down, to suddenly see them standing! Only underneath he was just the same. A little less sulky, she thought, and a great deal happier, but just the same!

Peter kissed her on her left cheek. "That's from me," he told her lightly. Then he kissed her on the right cheek. "And that's from my mother."

She kissed him back warmly. "I knew you'd do it!" she laughed in triumph. "But so soon! Oh, Peter, I am so pleased for you!"

Peter exchanged glances with his father. "I knew you would be!" he said.

"I should hope so!" she retorted.

He grinned. "Even if I hadn't, Piran made sure that I knew how much I owe to you!" he went on cheerfully.

"Oh?"

"Didn't you know?" he smiled. "We went to visit my mother's grave together last week."

"I'm glad," she said gently.

"It was the first time – since it happened, that we were on the same side, if you know what I mean?"

"Yes, I know," she said.

"You might say that we buried her together," Piran put in diffidently. "We should have done it before, but I didn't know Wendy's part in the affair – then!"

Peter made a face at the mention of her name. "Has she gone yet?" he inquired.

Piran nodded. "I made sure of that!" he answered with a touch of bitterness. "She'd done enough damage to me and mine!"

Anna gave him a quick look, blushed, and changed the subject. "How long have you been walking?" she asked him.

"If you can call it walking!" he retorted. "But it's grand to be on my feet again! I hadn't realised how small you are," he added teasingly.

"Thank you very much!" she exclaimed. "I hadn't realised how *big* you are!" she confessed.

They all laughed. Piran gathered up Peter's luggage, giving the car attendant a handsome tip for looking after the boy.

"Shall we go?" he asked them.

Peter nodded with determination. He was not entirely used to his crutches yet and he could only go very slowly. Yet he was making progress with every step he took and he was thoroughly pleased with his own performance.

"I think you'll have to admit," he said to Anna as they gained the car, "that Trethowyn fortitude is catching up with the St. James' brand!"

"Willingly!" she laughed. "Up the Trethowyns for ever!"

He gave her a hard, excited look. "Do you really mean that?" he demanded.

She was embarrassed. "Why not?" she said.

"You sound quite as if you were one of us!" he told her slyly.

Anna was considerably shaken as she got into the car. She was glad that she had the back to herself, for they had come in the smaller car and so Peter was able to sit in the front beside his father. The sooner she went away the better, she thought. If she stayed any longer, she would give herself away and Piran would feel sorry for her. She wanted his pity even less than she wanted his kindness. A dignified retreat was all that was left to her.

It was early enough for the streets of Penzance to be reasonably empty. Piran drove with care through the one-way system and up the hill.

"It's good to be home!" Peter breathed. "It's funny how much I wanted to go to London. I hated it when I got there!"

"Then you won't mind looking round the Meadhouse on your own this afternoon," his father told him. "I'm taking Anna out – by ourselves!"

The boy grinned. "I don't mind at all. I have an interest in this outing, don't forget!"

"I'm not sure that I can go," Anna said primly from the back. "It's the first I've heard of it –"

"Oh, Anna!" Piran said sadly. "Didn't I tell you it would all be different when the boy came home?"

Anna sat up very straight. "I don't remember," she mumbled.

"Oh, Anna!" he said again.

She was left in a state of confusion that neither Trethowyn did anything to clear up. They began to talk about the Mead House and complicated financial arrangements. Anna tried very hard not to think at all. The only thing she could remember about the conversation she had had with Piran was something about mourning for a ghost! He couldn't have meant it, she decided, for people did not mourn for ghosts.

They had reached the house before she connected the ghost with Caroline. Was *that* what he had been talking about? She tried to remember exactly what he had said. He had called her a loving ghost, she remembered that. An insubstantial ghost who mustn't be allowed to come between them in the future!

"I – I think I'll go straight home," she said immediately they had got out of the car. "You have a lot to talk about –"

"As long as you'll come this afternoon?" Piran said promptly.

Her eyes met his and she blushed.

178

"Well?"

"Yes. I – I'll come," she promised.

It was a very long morning. Anna started half a dozen different jobs and left them all unfinished. She went to the door and looked out, recognising the golden beauty of the day. The air was like champagne, for the humidity that was so often in the air when the sun was shining had gone. The whole of Mount's Bay was clearly visible, more beautiful than ever, with the sea dancing in the sunlight.

But even the view could not satisfy the restless, palpitating mood that Anna found herself in. She would be very well mannered and dignified that afternoon, she told herself. He might not mean anything more than a pleasant outing to reward her for all that she had suffered at Wendy's hands. It was more than possible that he meant nothing more than that! All this talk of ghosts had gone to his head – and yet Peter had said that they had visited Caroline's grave together. Perhaps Piran had owed it to his dead wife to mourn her as his anger had not allowed him to when she had died. Anna could not bring herself to resent his giving her those few days while Peter had been in London.

Of course she had never known Caroline. She had a vivid picture of her in her mind's eye, but that was not the same thing. For a little while she had been jealous of her, but now she only felt sad for her. Poor Caroline! She had lost so much: her husband, her son, life itself. And all because of the scheming of an evil woman.

No, Caroline was indeed a kindly ghost, the shadow of a woman beset and betrayed even by her own brother and the woman who had befriended her. But she was Peter's mother. No one could take that away from her. And Peter was the heir of the Trethowyns – Piran's heir. Anna sighed. Her own children could never be that, for Peter would always be the eldest son.

Anna checked her thoughts with an effort. It was terrible how one's mind could run on in this way. *Her* children indeed! And how could she ever resent Peter? He was very dear to her and far too like Piran for her to do anything else but love him!

She got herself some lunch, but she had no idea of what she ate. Then Piran was there, knocking on her door, and the endless morning had been all too short for her to prepare herself to meet him.

Piran was perfectly self-possessed. "I thought we wouldn't visit the Ding-Dong mine," he greeted her dryly.

Anna shook inside. "N-no," she said.

Piran came into the cabin and shut the door behind him. Anna took a step backwards into the hearth, spreading her hands against her skirts.

"I – I'm quite ready!" she informed him brightly.

Piran smiled slowly. "Are you?" he teased her.

She wished she wasn't so given to blushing. "Peter looks very well, doesn't he?" she said.

"Very well," Piran agreed.

"I hadn't realised he's so tall," she went on conversationally.

Piran came into the hearth too and sat down, looking up at her with laughing eyes. "Are we going to talk about Peter all afternoon?" he asked her.

Anna swallowed. "N-not if you don't want to."

"I don't," he confirmed.

Anna thought about this for a minute. "What do you want to talk about?" she asked him.

He laughed. It was clear that he was enjoying himself very much.

"Shall we begin with you?" he suggested.

180

"If you like," Anna said with difficulty.

"Tell me about your life in London," he said.

"There isn't much to tell." She blushed again, remembering what he had said about all pretty girls liking a gay life. How could she persuade him that hers hadn't been at all like that? "It was mostly work," she said. "I had my mother to look after as well."

"But then she died?"

Anna nodded. "She was a Cornish woman by birth, but apart from the occasional holiday, she had hardly ever been to Cornwall. It was because of her that I wanted to come."

"I can understand that," he agreed, "but then I'm Cornish through and through. I've never lived anywhere else but here in the same house. Does that seem dull to you?"

She shook her head. "It must be nice to have roots like that," she said simply. "The St. Jameses have never had anywhere much to call their own!"

Piran threw back his head and laughed. "Do I detect a note of envy?" he accused her. "Have the Trethowyns something that the St. Jameses have not?"

Anna made an effort to look dignified. She sank down on to the settle, pretending that she didn't know he was teasing her. "Why not?" she said.

He laughed again. "I don't want you to think you're giving up anything by becoming a Trethowyn," he said gently.

Anna refused to meet his eyes. "I think we're talking a great deal of nonsense," she said with resolution. "If we're going out, don't you think we ought to be going?"

"Why, Anna, I believe you're afraid!" he challenged her.

"I am not!" she retorted, clutching her hands together lest they should betray her by trembling. "Why should I be?"

"Why indeed?"

He stood up, pulling her to her feet as well, and into his

arms. She gulped nervously, trying vainly to free herself. "It isn't fair!" she complained.

"Isn't it?"

His arms were pleasantly warm around her, but his dark, laughing face still frightened her. He kissed her very gently on the lips and her resolutions to be dignified and very sure before she committed herself died on the spot.

"Oh, Piran!" she sobbed.

"That's much better!" he said with all the arrogance that she associated with him.

But it wasn't better at all. When he kissed her, Anna couldn't think at all. Her heart leaped within her and she was straining closer that he might kiss her again more easily.

"Oh dear," she said when he released her. "I hadn't meant that to happen at all!"

"Hadn't you?" he said in her ear. "Why not?"

"I – I –"

"You *like* it!" he reminded her.

"That isn't the point!" She struggled valiantly to sort out in her mind just what the point was, but failed dismally.

"My darling love," Piran said lovingly.

"D-don't!" Anna managed.

"Don't what?"

"Don't kiss me again!"

"But I *like* kissing you!" he complained.

She pulled herself free of him, in a state of great agitation. She licked her lips and ran an anxious hand through her hair. "But liking isn't enough!"

His eyes danced. "I can see you've thought it all out," he agreed gravely. "What would be enough?"

"I'd have to be sure," she insisted. "Caroline thought you loved her, but in the end she wasn't sure at all!"

The laughter in his eyes died. "Caroline is dead," he said abruptly.

"But she didn't *know*!" Anna said again unhappily.

"I shan't make that mistake a second time," he told her harshly. "Anna St. James will be in no doubt whatever that she's loved. I promise you that!"

Anna's eyes sought his, seeking reassurance. "You see," she said bravely, "I'm so very much in love with you that I couldn't bear it if I didn't know –"

"You'll know!" he shot at her. "Oh, Anna, how could you ever doubt it? Don't you know that I love you? Didn't you know it when I first kissed you on Lizard Point?"

She shook her head. "How could I?" she said.

He looked amused. "My dear, that kind of kiss is rare indeed!"

"I knew that!" she assured him. "But I didn't know that you loved me. I was still shocked by the knowledge that I loved *you*! And you said –"

"Something foolish, no doubt!" he sighed.

"You said that I must be missing my gay life in London and that all women are the same. You even said that I probably liked Michael to kiss me too! And I don't know how you could, because I disliked him more than I could say!"

"I must have been mad!" he confessed with a chuckle.

"D-didn't you mean it?" she asked him diffidently.

"I was angry," he tried to explain. "I'd had enough of women to last me a long time – Wendy as well as Caroline! And then you came along with a dusting of freckles on your nose, and a sublime indifference as to what any Trethowyn might think of you. I'm surprised I didn't wring your neck!"

Anna was faintly shocked. She had not thought it went as deeply with him as that!

"I – I only wanted to jolt Peter into *trying* to walk again."

she explained quickly. "I don't really think the St. James brand of courage is better. I thought you knew that."

He laughed. "You gave me precious little reason to know!" he exclaimed.

"Oh!" said Anna. "I thought I'd given you *every* reason to know! I couldn't even deny it when you asked me if I liked your kissing me!"

"No," he remembered with complacent pleasure. "As a matter of fact, I thought that was pretty courageous of you, my love!"

"Well, I wasn't prepared to lie about it," she said gruffly. "You see, I'd never really been kissed before. It makes one very vulnerable –"

He leaned forward and kissed her lips. "Like that?" he asked.

"No, not like that at all!" she retorted. She came happily into his arms. "Piran, I love you so very much!" she said.

He grinned. "I know," he said. And he kissed her again.

It was a long time before they spoke again. Anna thought she had never known such bliss as to love Piran and to know that she was loved by him. She had not known that love could be violent, a perilous voyage towards delight, but it was what she had wanted, it seemed for ever. There was nothing *kind* about Piran's kisses – nor in her response! It was more like a match flaring into life, a conflagration that caught her unawares, releasing a burning, passionate nature she had not known she possessed.

"This won't do!" she said at last.

"No?" he murmured. "Kiss me again!"

She did so. "We must be sensible," she protested. She made a movement to tidy her hair. "What we need is a cup of tea," she said firmly.

He watched her lazily. "Does that mean you really do want to go out?" he asked her.

Anna blushed. "N-not particularly," she admitted. She pulled herself right away from him to the other side of the room. The old hearth would never look quite the same to her, she thought. It held a radiance that other eyes would never see, but which would always be there for her. "I'll make us some tea," she said.

There was something satisfying about going through the familiar movements of making tea. She measured the leaves into the teapot and poured on the boiling water almost as if she were in a dream.

When she carried the tray into the sitting-room, Piran was standing in the hearth, examining the Cornish cross of St. Piran she had bought in Lizard Town.

"I see it has a place of honour," he said with a smile.

She smiled back. "It holds a very special memory for me," she said. She put the tray down on a small table and sat down on the settle. She knew so little about Piran, she thought. She didn't even know if he took sugar in his tea!

"I don't," he said, reading her thoughts.

"Just as well," she answered, "I forgot to put it on the tray." She handed him a cup of tea with a smile.

"I had meant to take you into Penzance to choose a ring," he told her suddenly. "But I was overcome with nerves when I thought about the stuff you turn out. Am I right in thinking that the orthodox diamond would seem a bit to you?"

Anna had never thought about an engagement ring for herself. "I – I don't know," she said. She looked up at him, delighting in the firm lines of his face and the way his hair curled into his neck. "I think I'd like anything you gave me!"

His eyebrows shot up. "How are the mighty fallen!" he teased her.

185

She smiled. "I admit it! I even rather like it," she admitted.

He fumbled in his pocket and produced a small curved box, the kind that jewellers pack rings in, in white silk. "I have this ring," he said apologetically. "We've had it in the family for at least two centuries. I don't think it has much value otherwise –"

"Let me see it!" Anna demanded.

He opened it slowly, a little ashamed of what he was offering her. "If you don't like it –" he began.

"Don't like it!" Anna repeated. "Oh, Piran, I think it's beautiful!"

He picked out the ring and pushed it on to her finger. It had a Georgian look about it, with a solid silver setting. The stone itself was black, the pure black of jet, with a silver cross etched into it – the cross of St. Piran and Cornwall.

Anna tried to blink away the tears before Piran could see them. It was so like him! With a flicker of amusement, she thought it was almost like wearing his personal brand!

"There's no need to cry about it!" he told her anxiously. "If you want a new ring, you shall have one."

"Oh no!" she exclaimed. "I shall never want anyone but this!"

"You're sure?"

She reached up and kissed the doubt out of his eyes. "Darling, can't you see I love it?"

He bent his head. "It's a long time since the last time it was worn," he told her. "It comes to you with much love – from both the Trethowyns."

Anna reached up and kissed him. "My dear, I love you! I'm – I'm –" She sought in her mind for the right words – "I'm *honoured* to wear it," she said at last.

He looked amused. "That's what Peter said you'd say," he told her.

She was immediately indignant. "Peter? What does he know about it?"

Piran kissed her gently on the nose. "More than we think!" he retorted with laughter. "He can't wait for me to make you a Trethowyn!"

Anna smiled ruefully. "Neither can I!" she confessed.

Each month from Harlequin

8 NEW FULL LENGTH ROMANCE NOVELS

Listed below are the last three months' releases:

FREE!!!

Did you know.....?

that just by mailing in the coupon below you can receive a brand new, up-to-date "Harlequin Romance Catalogue" listing literally hundreds of Harlequin Romances you probably thought were out of print.

Now you can shop in your own home for novels by your favorite Harlequin authors — the Essie Summers you wanted to read, the Violet Winspear you missed, the Mary Burchell you thought wasn't available anymore!

They're all listed in the "Harlequin Romance Catalogue". And something else too — the books are listed in numerical sequence, — so you can fill in the missing numbers in your library.

Don't delay — mail the coupon below to us today. We'll promptly send you the "Harlequin Romance Catalogue".

Have You Missed Any of These
Harlequin Romances?

- [ ] 427 NURSE BROOKES
  Kate Norway
- [ ] 438 MASTER OF SURGERY
  Alex Stuart
- [ ] 446 TO PLEASE THE DOCTOR
  Marjorie Moore
- [ ] 458 NEXT PATIENT, DOCTOR
  ANNE, Elizabeth Gilzean
- [ ] 468 SURGEON OF DISTINCTION
  Mary Burchell
- [ ] 469 MAGGY, Sara Seale
- [ ] 486 NURSE CARIL'S NEW POST
  Caroline Trench
- [ ] 487 THE HAPPY ENTERPRISE
  Eleanor Farnes
- [ ] 491 NURSE TENNANT
  Elizabeth Hoy
- [ ] 494 LOVE IS MY REASON
  Mary Burchell
- [ ] 495 NURSE WITH A DREAM
  Norrey Ford
- [ ] 503 NURSE IN CHARGE
  Elizabeth Gilzean
- [ ] 504 PETER RAYNAL, SURGEON
  Marjorie Moore
- [ ] 584 VILLAGE HOSPITAL
  Margaret Malcolm
- [ ] 599 RUN AWAY FROM LOVE
  Jean S. Macleod
  (Original Harlequin title
  "Nurse Companion")
- [ ] 631 DOCTOR'S HOUSE
  Dorothy Rivers
- [ ] 647 JUNGLE HOSPITAL
  Juliet Shore
- [ ] 672 GREGOR LOTHIAN, SURGEON
  Joan Blair
- [ ] 683 DESIRE FOR THE STAR
  Averil Ives
  (Original Harlequin title
  "Doctor's Desire")
- [ ] 744 VERENA FAYRE, PROBA-
  TIONER, Valerie K. Nelson
- [ ] 745 TENDER NURSE, Hilda Nickson
- [ ] 757 THE PALM-THATCHED
  HOSPITAL. Juliet Shore
- [ ] 758 HELPING DOCTOR MEDWAY
  Jan Haye
- [ ] 764 NURSE ANN WOOD
  Valerie K. Nelson

- [ ] 771 NURSE PRUE IN CEYLON
  Gladys Fullbrook
- [ ] 772 CHLOE WILDE, STUDENT
  NURSE, Joan Turner
- [ ] 787 THE TWO FACES OF NURSE
  ROBERTS, Nora Sanderson
- [ ] 790 SOUTH TO THE SUN
  Betty Beaty
- [ ] 794 SURGEON'S RETURN
  Hilda Nickson
- [ ] 812 FACTORY NURSE   Hilary Neal
- [ ] 825 MAKE UP YOUR MIND NURSE
  Phyllis Matthewman
- [ ] 841 TRUANT HEART
  Patricia Fenwick
  (Original Harlequin title
  "Doctor in Brazil")
- [ ] 858 MY SURGEON NEIGHBOUR
  Jane Arbor
- [ ] 873 NURSE JULIE OF WARD
  THREE   Joan Callender
- [ ] 878 THIS KIND OF LOVE
  Kathryn Blair
- [ ] 890 TWO SISTERS
  Valerie K. Nelson
- [ ] 897 NURSE HILARY'S HOLIDAY
  TASK, Jan Haye
- [ ] 900 THERE CAME A SURGEON
  Hilda Pressley
- [ ] 901 HOPE FOR TOMORROW
  Anne Weale
- [ ] 902 MOUNTAIN OF DREAMS
  Barbara Rowan
- [ ] 903 SO LOVED AND SO FAR
  Elizabeth Hoy
- [ ] 907 HOMECOMING HEART
  Joan Blair
  (Original Harlequin title
  "Two for the Doctor")
- [ ] 909 DESERT DOORWAY
  Pamela Kent
- [ ] 911 RETURN OF SIMON
  Celine Conway
- [ ] 912 THE DREAM AND THE
  DANCER, Eleanor Farnes
- [ ] 919 DEAR INTRUDER
  Jane Arbor
- [ ] 936 TIGER HALL
  Esther Wyndham

PLEASE NOTE: All Harlequin Romances from #1857
onwards are 75c. Books below that number, **where avail-
able** are priced at 60c through Harlequin Reader Service
until December 31st, 1975.

AA

Have You Missed Any of These Harlequin Romances?

Have You Missed Any of These
Harlequin Romances?

☐ 1246 THE CONSTANT HEART
  Eleanor Farnes
☐ 1248 WHERE LOVE IS
  Norrey Ford
☐ 1253 DREAM COME TRUE
  Patricia Fenwick
☐ 1276 STEEPLE RIDGE
  Jill Tahourdin
☐ 1277 STRANGER'S TRESPASS
  Jane Arbor
☐ 1282 THE SHINING STAR
  Hilary Wilde
☐ 1284 ONLY MY HEART TO GIVE
  Nan Asquith
☐ 1288 THE LAST OF THE KINTYRES
  Catherine Airlie
☐ 1293 I KNOW MY LOVE
  Sara Seale
☐ 1309 THE HILLS OF MAKETU
  Gloria Bevan
☐ 1312 PEPPERCORN HARVEST
  Ivy Ferrari
☐ 1601 THE NEWCOMER
  Hilda Pressley
☐ 1607 NOT LESS THAN ALL
  Margaret Malcolm
☐ 1718 LORD OF THE FOREST
  Hilda Nickson
☐ 1722 FOLLOW A STRANGER
  Charlotte Lamb
☐ 1725 THE EXTRAORDINARY EN-
  GAGEMENT Marjorie Lewty
☐ 1726 MAN IN CHARGE, Lilian Feake
☐ 1729 THE YOUNG DOCTOR
  Sheila Douglas
☐ 1730 FLAME IN FIJI, Gloria Bevan
☐ 1731 THE FORBIDDEN VALLEY
  Essie Summers
☐ 1732 BEYOND THE SUNSET
  Flora Kidd
☐ 1733 CALL AND I'LL COME
  Mary Burchell
☐ 1734 THE GIRL FROM ROME
  Nan Asquith
☐ 1735 TEMPTATIONS OF THE MOON
  Hilary Wilde
☐ 1736 THE ENCHANTED RING
  Lucy Gillen

☐ 1737 WINTER OF CHANGE
  Betty Neels
☐ 1738 THE MUTUAL LOOK
  Joyce Dingwell
☐ 1739 BELOVED ENEMY
  Mary Wibberley
☐ 1740 ROMAN SUMMER
  Jane Arbor
☐ 1741 MOORLAND MAGIC
  Elizabeth Ashton
☐ 1743 DESTINY IS A FLOWER
  Stella Frances Nel
☐ 1744 WINTER LOVING
  Janice Gray
☐ 1745 NURSE AT NOONGWALLA
  Roumelia Lane
☐ 1746 WITHOUT ANY AMAZEMENT
  Margaret Malcolm
☐ 1748 THE GOLDEN MADONNA
  Rebecca Stratton
☐ 1749 LOVELY IS THE ROSE
  Belinda Dell
☐ 1750 THE HOUSE OF THE SCISSORS
  Isobel Chace
☐ 1751 CARNIVAL COAST
  Charlotte Lamb
☐ 1752 MIRANDA'S MARRIAGE
  Margery Hilton
☐ 1753 TIME MAY CHANGE
  Nan Asquith
☐ 1754 THE PRETTY WITCH
  Lucy Gillen
☐ 1755 SCHOOL MY HEART
  Penelope Walsh
☐ 1756 AN APPLE IN EDEN
  Kay Thorpe
☐ 1757 THE GIRL AT SALTBUSH FLAT
  Dorothy Cork
☐ 1758 THE CRESCENT MOON
  Elizabeth Hunter
☐ 1759 THE REST IS MAGIC
  Marjorie Lewty
☐ 1760 THE GUARDED GATES
  Katrina Britt
☐ 1780 THE TOWER OF THE WINDS
  Elizabeth Hunter
☐ 1783 CINDERELLA IN MINK
  Roberta Leigh

PLEASE NOTE: All Harlequin Romances from #1857 onwards are 75c. Books below that number, **where avail-able** are priced at 60c through Harlequin Reader Service until December 31st, 1975.

CC